It was all over now. Her only son, her beloved son, was condemned to death. For a crime she knew he could not have committed.

She gathered her strength for what she must do. From the pocket of her long skirt the old Gypsy pulled the bandanna with the objects. The pen. The crumpled paper cup. The metal tack.

None was of great value. But they held the power she needed. For each had belonged to one of the people she was going to curse tonight.

Her hand clenched the pen. "Justice is blind," she whispered, then joined the curse with the name of Wyatt Boudreaux.

"Love is death," she intoned as she crumpled the paper cup in her hand and said the name of Garner Rousseau.

Finally she picked up the tack and said, "The law is impotent," linking those words with the name of Andrei Sobatka.

Pushing herself erect, she stood and shuffled to the edge of the bayou, smug in her satisfaction that she had evened the score.

D0974872

Dear Harlequin Intrigue Reader,

The suspenseful tales we offer you this month are much scarier than Halloween's ghouls and ghosts! So bring out your trick-or-treating bag and gather up all four exciting stories.

And do we have a *treat* for you—a brand-new 3-in-1 compilation featuring authors Rebecca York, Ann Voss Peterson and Patricia Rosemoor. Ten years ago, three men were cursed by a Gypsy woman bent on vengeance. Now they must race to find a killer—and true love's kiss may just break the evil spell they're under in *Gypsy Magic*.

Next, Aimée Thurlo concludes her two-book miniseries SIGN OF THE GRAY WOLF, with *Navajo Justice*. And Susan Kearney starts a new trilogy, THE CROWN AFFAIR, in which royalty of the country of Vashmira must battle palace danger and treachery, while finding true love along the way. Look for *Royal Target* this month.

When Jennifer Ballard dreamed of her wedding day, it never included murder! But no one would harm the beautiful bride, not if Colby Agency investigator Ethan Delaney had anything to say about it. Pick up *Contract Bride* for yet another nail-biter from Debra Webb.

Happy reading!

Denise O'Sullivan
Associate Senior Editor
Harlequin Intrigue

GYPSY MAGIC

REBECCA YORK

RUTH GLICK WRITING AS REBECCA YORK

ANN VOSS PETERSON

PATRICIA ROSEMOOR

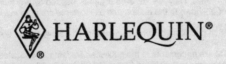

HARLEQUIN®

TORONTO • NEW YORK • LONDON
AMSTERDAM • PARIS • SYDNEY • HAMBURG
STOCKHOLM • ATHENS • TOKYO • MILAN • MADRID
PRAGUE • WARSAW • BUDAPEST • AUCKLAND

ISBN 0-373-22684-5

GYPSY MAGIC

Copyright © 2002 by Harlequin Books S.A.

The publisher acknowledges the copyright holders
of the individual works as follows:

ALESSANDRA
Copyright © 2002 by Ruth Glick

SABINA
Copyright © 2002 by Ann Voss Peterson

ANDREI
Copyright © 2002 by Patricia Pinianski

This edition published by arrangement with Harlequin Books S.A.

® and TM are trademarks of the publisher. Trademarks indicated with
® are registered in the United States Patent and Trademark Office, the
Canadian Trade Marks Office and in other countries.

Visit us at www.eHarlequin.com

Printed in U.S.A.

ABOUT THE AUTHORS

Award-winning, bestselling novelist **Ruth Glick, who writes as Rebecca York,** is the author of close to eighty books, including her popular 43 LIGHT STREET series for Harlequin Intrigue. Ruth says she has the best job in the world. Not only does she get paid for telling stores, she's also the author of twelve cookbooks. Ruth and her husband, Norman, travel frequently, researching locales for her novels and searching out new dishes for her cookbooks.

Ever since she was a little girl making her own books out of construction paper, **Ann Voss Peterson** wanted to write. So when it came time to choose a major at the University of Wisconsin, creative writing was the only choice. Of course, writing wasn't a *practical* choice—one needs to earn a living. So Ann found jobs ranging from proofreading legal transcripts to working with quarter horses to washing windows. But no matter how she earned her paycheck, she continued to write the type of stories that captured her heart and imagination—romantic suspense. Ann lives near Madison, Wisconsin, with her husband, her toddler son, her Border collie and her quarter horse mare.

To research her novels, **Patricia Rosemoor** is willing to swim with dolphins, round up mustangs or howl with wolves—"whatever it takes to write a credible tale." She's written in many genres, but her first love has always been romantic suspense. She won both a *Romantic Times* Career Achievement Award in Series Romantic Suspense and a Reviewer's Choice Award for one of her more than thirty Intrigue novels. She's now writing erotic thrillers for Harlequin Blaze. Ms. Rosemoor also teaches Suspense-Thriller and Popular Fiction writing at Columbia College Chicago. She lives in Chicago with her husband, Edward, and their three cats. She would love to know what you think of this story. Write to Patricia Rosemoor at P.O. Box 578297, Chicago, IL 60657-8297 or via e-mail at Patricia@PatriciaRosemoor.com, and visit her Web site at http://PatriciaRosemoor.com.

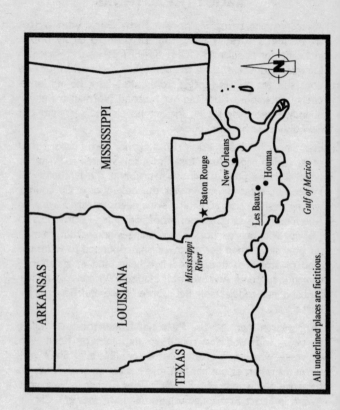

All underlined places are fictitious.

ALLESANDRA

REBECCA YORK

RUTH GLICK WRITING AS REBECCA YORK

To Norman, once more, with love.

Prologue

The old woman lifted her lantern, the dim glow flickering off the Spanish moss that trailed from the dark branches above her head.

Somewhere in the far reaches of the bayou, an animal called out. An animal whose pain echoed her own.

Sinking to her knees on the damp ground, she threw back her head and gave voice to her anguish. It was all over now. Her only son, her beloved son, was condemned to die. For a crime she knew he could not have committed. He had made mistakes. She had warned him of the consequences, but never in her wildest imagination had she thought it would come to this.

She let her tears flow then. Tears of anger and regret. And when the storm of weeping finally subsided, she gathered her strength for what she must do. From the pocket of her long skirt, she pulled the bandanna with the objects. The pen. The paper cup. The metal tack.

Spreading the cloth on the ground, she stared at the tokens she had stolen. None was of material value. But they held the power she needed. For each belonged to one of the people she was going to curse tonight.

With bony fingers she touched each object in turn, calling on her inner strength, summoning the dark powers she had learned to control long ago.

For she had the Romany gift of turning the tables on her enemies. She'd done it since she was a child. For small offenses and large, yet never anything so large as this.

Her enemies had taken her most precious possession—her son. He was lost to her now. Lost by trickery and deceit. But the three people who had cut out her heart would pay in kind. They would feel the pain she had felt. For they each had a son: Wyatt Boudreaux, Garner Rousseau, Andrei Sobatka. And each would suffer a fate worse than death. A fate that would follow him till the end of his days.

In a low voice she began to chant the ancient words of her people, weaving in a curse for each man as she conjured up his face.

Her hand clenched the pen. "Justice is blind," she whispered, then joined the curse with the name of Wyatt Boudreaux.

"Love is death," she intoned as she crumpled the paper cup in her hand and said the name of Garner Rousseau.

Finally she picked up the tack, her finger caressing the cold metal as she said, "The law is impotent," then linked the name with Andrei Sobatka.

Three times more she repeated the ritual before gathering up the objects in her bandanna and knotting the ends. Pushing herself erect, she stood swaying on unsteady legs, then shuffled to the bayou edge where cypress knees jutted like gravestones from the dark water. She tossed the bundle into the murky depths, watching it sink before she turned, picked up her lantern and walked back through the humid darkness to her trailer, smug in her satisfaction that she had evened the score.

Chapter One

Ten years later...

The Gypsy carnival had returned to Les Baux, Louisiana, as it did every summer. For the past four years, Wyatt Boudreaux had avoided the place the way an alligator trapper avoids quicksand pits.

Now he was back—for his dying father's sake.

"Wait right here for me," he said to the cabdriver. "I won't be much more than an hour."

"It's your nickel." Henry Beaver answered. Henry was one of only two cabbies in Les Baux, which meant that he and Wyatt had an ongoing relationship. A love-hate relationship.

The humid evening air pressed around Wyatt like damp cotton. The old Ford wasn't air-conditioned, and he could already feel his white dress shirt sticking to his back.

With a sigh, he climbed out and turned toward the noise of the midway. A tall, muscular man with dark hair, blue eyes and a scar that pierced his soul, he stood for a moment taking in the carnival spread out at the edge of town along the bayou's low bank.

He heard the delighted squeals of children, the screams

of teenagers riding the Tilt-a-Whirl, the Gypsy barkers urging people to try the games of chance. Beneath the running shoes he almost always wore, he felt the layer of wood chips spread over the grass. On a deep breath, he dragged in the aromas of cotton candy, roasting hot dogs and fried dough.

"Hey, you're blocking the entrance, mister," a boy complained. He sounded like he was about eight.

"Son, that's not polite," a man said—probably when he noticed Wyatt's dark glasses and the white cane he held.

"Sorry," the boy mumbled.

Wyatt swallowed to dislodge the knot in his throat as he moved to one side. "No problem."

Sura May LePage, one of his research assistants, had scanned the newspaper's map of the midway into his computer. Then his special software had read him the locations of the various attractions. He'd memorized the layout so he could find his way around.

But he wasn't here for pleasure. He was here because his father had been chief investigator on the "Gypsy murder" case that had captured the headlines in the *Les Baux Record* ten years ago. Carlo Mustov, a rough and belligerent carny, had murdered Theresa Granville, the wife of one of the town's most prominent citizens—Mayor Richard Granville. After finally exhausting his appeals, Carlo was scheduled to die in the state penitentiary in Angola next month. And Dad wanted to make sure nobody screwed up the process.

Wyatt couldn't hold back a sardonic laugh. Of course, by sending his son on this mission, his father was sending the wrong man. Two years ago Wyatt had been a top detective on the New Orleans police force. Now...now he kept himself sharp by working on old cases and lending his expertise to the local police force, which was why he knew nobody else was going to poke into the Gypsy murder case anytime soon. Everybody considered it a done deal—except Dad—who seemed to have some nagging fears that Wyatt couldn't understand.

But he *could* reassure his dying father that the carnies were going to keep their noses out of it. He'd speak to Milo Vasilli, the owner. Milo was one of the Gypsies, but he'd played straight with the cops on this case—to avoid trouble with the town. Maybe he'd even been secretly relieved that Carlo was out of the way, since the young man had been a troublemaker—a thorn in his side.

Using his cane to identify obstructions, Wyatt started down the midway, counting off the paces, picturing the noisy crowd around him and the various tents and concession stands as he passed them. He had some minimal vision left—a sense of light and dark—so he could detect where the temporary structures blocked the lights strung above the carnival grounds.

About halfway down the midway, bodies pushed against him, and he was pretty sure that laughing teenagers were having some fun with the blind man.

He had time for a flash of anger before he lost his footing and dropped his cane. Instinctively he caught the edge of a tent flap with his hands.

The boys moved on. He was alone. With a sigh, he started to search for the cane when the scent of perfume wafted toward him, and he went absolutely still. Damn. Fate had literally pushed him into the fortune-teller's tent. In his mind he pictured the interior—opulent with bright hangings, fringed pillows and a velvet-covered table.

He felt his stomach clench, but the tent appeared to be empty. Thank God. Reaching behind himself, he felt for the opening. He had almost made his escape when he heard fabric rustling, then a woman's indrawn breath.

"Wyatt?"

He squeezed his eyes shut, struggling to blot out the image of Alessandra King that formed in his mind. But it was no use. He could picture her perfectly. She'd be wearing a flowing, scooped neck dress swirling with bright colors. Her wavy hair would be loose around her shoulders, and the gold hoops on her ears would swing gently when she turned her head.

"You have your nerve coming here," she said, her voice etched with acid.

Her voice told him two things. She hadn't forgiven him for being Louis Boudreaux's son, and she couldn't tell that his eyes were blind behind his dark glasses.

"My mistake," he said, his fingers clutching the tent flap. The cane was still on the ground. He'd leave it there. Let her think someone else had dropped it. He could make it back up the midway, climb into Henry Beaver's cab and get the hell out of here. Tomorrow he'd contact Vasilli by phone.

Needing desperately to put distance between himself and this woman, he turned too quickly. His foot caught the edge of a rug, and he pitched forward, his glasses flying off, then crunching under his shoe.

Alessandra must have stepped quickly forward and stopped his fall, because he landed solidly against her body, her breasts crushed against his chest, her hands clutching his arms.

He was a big man, and she was delicately made. He felt her stagger backward even as he held on to her to stay erect, held on to womanly softness and feminine curves.

Smooth move, Boudreaux, he thought just before his whole world turned upside down. Not literally, this time.

Incredibly, a flash of vision came to him. An illusion, it must be, because there was no other way to explain what was happening. It was as though he was seeing again. But not through his own eyes. In a moment of startling clarity, he saw his own contorted face, saw the pain and humiliation.

His hand brushed a horizontal surface, which he recognized as the back of a chair. Grabbing on, he straightened as he pulled himself away from her. When the contact snapped, so did the moment of sight.

He stood stunned and panting, trying and failing to wrap his head around what had just happened. He heard her sharply indrawn breath.

"You're blind," she whispered. Then with a kind of terrible deadness in her voice, "Wyatt, are you blind?"

"Yeah." He kept his face defiantly turned toward her so she could see him in all his glory.

"How? What happened?"

"I got shot in the head by a drug dealer," he tossed off, profoundly glad that he couldn't see the pity he heard in her voice. "They give you a nice pension when you get disabled in the line of duty."

"I'm sorry."

He shrugged. "Don't be. It wasn't your fault. You know, like Carlo wasn't my fault," he couldn't stop himself from saying, then wondered why he'd felt compelled to hurt her.

The man's name hung in the perfumed air, bringing back all the old wounds. He and Alessandra had met five years ago when he'd come to the carnival to have some fun and ended up saving her from a robbery attempt. They'd been drawn to each other and had subsequently gotten close. For six weeks, he'd spent all his free time following the carnival, even though he'd been afraid that a permanent relationship between them was hopeless. She was too tied to her family—to her sister who was recovering from some kind of tragedy. She was a Gypsy. He was an outsider. Her people were close-knit, suspicious of his intentions, because they had been misunderstood and persecuted through the ages. He'd understood that, tried to make them see he was different.

Then, to his horror, he'd found out she was Carlo Mustov's cousin. Before he could figure out what to say to her about that, one of the carnies had solved the problem for him—by telling her that man she was seeing was the son of the police officer who had collected the evidence against Carlo.

She'd come at Wyatt with fire in her eyes and a curse on her lips, saying he'd tricked her, saying he was the worst kind of scum.

There had been no reasoning with her. Heartsick, he'd left the carnival. Later he'd realized that he must have been delusional if he'd thought there could be anything meaningful between them.

Now here they were, facing each other again. And he was fighting all the old feelings he'd told himself were dead.

All at once he ached to stay here with her—at least for a little while. "So are you going to tell my fortune?" he heard himself say. She'd never done it before, because his future had been twined with hers, which she had never been able to see. Now everything was different.

"Wyatt...don't ask that," she said with a softness that startled him.

"Why not? Isn't my money good here?" He reached into his pocket and pulled out his wallet. The bills were each folded differently so he could identify them. Pulling out a twenty, he held it toward her.

"That's too much," she whispered.

"I didn't make a mistake. I know it's a twenty," he snapped. "You're supposed to be good at your job. Prove it!"

He heard her small gasp and knew he had hurt her again, but still he stood there. Finally he heard her chair scrape back, heard the swish of her long skirt as she sat.

He pulled out the chair he'd gripped earlier and seated himself across from her.

"Do you want me to read the Tarot cards? Or look into my crystal ball?" she asked in a low voice.

"I want you to read my palm," he said, laying his hand on the velvet surface of the table.

He waited for her to refuse. Then her small hand cupped his larger one—and he was swept into a vortex of feelings. The softness of her. Desire he couldn't entirely shut out, even when he fought it with every fiber of his being.

Then it happened again. The same startling experience that had stunned and confused him moments before. She touched him, and once more he caught a flash of vision. Of sight. So ordinary and yet so beyond his reach. This time he had the sensation of staring down into his own rough, callused hand.

He felt her go rigid, felt her drop his hand.

"You bastard," she spat.

Chapter Two

"I know why you came here," she said, her voice rising in anger.

"Why?" he challenged.

"Your damn father sent you. He wants to make sure that none of the nasty Gypsies make trouble. He wants to make sure that Carlo dies for a crime he didn't commit."

"That's wrong!" he responded automatically.

"Don't lie to me, *gadjo*."

"I'm not lying! I mean, you're right, my father sent me. He's dying, in case you didn't pick that up, and he wants this case finally wrapped up. The evidence—"

"Was false," she interrupted. "Your father wanted Carlo convicted and he made sure it happened."

"No."

"Get out of here. I can't stand the sight of you."

"I wish I could say the same," he answered, and had the satisfaction of hearing her make a small, strangled sound. "I don't need you to feel sorry for me," he added. "Just find my cane for me. I dropped it when some boys pushed me in here. It's probably over by the door. Forget the glasses. I'm pretty sure I stepped on them."

He heard her move across the tent, waited for the span

of heartbeats while she searched the ground. Then she was back, and he felt the handle of the cane touch his wrist.

"Thank you," he said, wrapping his fist around the hard plastic. I won't bother you again. My father was quite agitated when I left him in the hospital. I'd like him to die in peace, so perhaps you could ask Milo Vasilli to call me. I'm living here in town now." Fishing in his pocket, he pulled out one of his business cards and tossed it in the direction of the table.

Without waiting for a response, he turned and walked rapidly out of the tent, then stood in the damp night air, breathing hard, as if he'd just run the hundred-yard dash.

Inside, he'd had the sensation of being shut away with Alessandra—just the two of them. Now the sounds and smells of the carnival washed over him once more. Was Alessandra standing in there, watching him? Or had she turned away?

His insides knotted, and he ordered himself to put her out of his mind. Deliberately he considered how to get back to the parking lot. He'd turned right when he walked down the midway. Now he turned left, making his way as quickly as possible toward the entrance, feeling the crowd part like the Red Sea before his white cane.

He discovered quickly that Henry Beaver hadn't waited for him. Probably people had emerged from the carnival wanting a ride—and Henry had obliged them. Then again, maybe he'd gone down to the Blue Heron bar. That was one of the problems with depending on Henry. The old coot was several shades less than reliable. And a bad driver, to boot, judging from the squeal of breaks he heard from the other vehicles as they tooled around town.

Wyatt walked back to the midway, considering what to do next. There were still plenty of people around him, but which of them would know where to find a phone in this unfamiliar environment?

He could hear a barker working one of the booths—the ring toss, he gathered from the guy's spiel.

"Try your luck. Win one of these fabulous prizes. You sir—win a giant teddy bear for the little lady."

In his mind, he pictured the barker. Probably in his twenties or thirties. A sincere smile that didn't reach his eyes.

As he listened, the "little lady" squealed her approval. Wyatt waited while the sucker made the toss. He gathered from the ensuing disappointed noises that the effort had been a failure.

In the lull that followed, he stepped up to the booth.

"Try your luck—" The guy stopped abruptly. No doubt he'd seen the white cane.

Wyatt fixed his empty gaze on the man. "Can you direct me to a public phone?"

There was a half-second pause. "Past the next couple of booths. Turn right."

"You're sure about that?"

"Absolutely," the barker snapped. "I just had to think where they'd put it when we set up."

"Okay. Thanks." Right, Wyatt thought. The next couple of booths. Using his sense of light and dark, he detected their shapes, moved past them. His hearing had always been good, and the crowd was thinning out now. The people around him were less a mass of sounds, the individual voices more distinct. He'd make it to the phone with no problem.

FOR LONG MOMENTS, Alessandra stood as though turned to stone. Wyatt Boudreaux! He was here. She'd touched him. Held him in her arms, in fact, when he'd started to

fall. Now she couldn't catch her breath. She was too
shocked. Too confused.

Wyatt Boudreaux. Blind. But not bowed. Changed. Bitter. Angry. Yet when she had held his hand, she had felt
all the old emotions below the surface, emotions she
hadn't been able to deal with five years ago and certainly
couldn't deal with now. Despite everything, he still
wanted her, and that was almost too much to bear.

Her loyalty was to her family. To Sabina. To Carlo. To
the Romany band who had nurtured her since she was a
little girl. People who stood together and protected their
own.

Wyatt had lied to her. Well, not in so many words. But
he'd known his father was the detective who had worked
to convict Carlo. And he hadn't mentioned that little fact
to her. She'd told herself she hated him. She'd tried to
convince herself it was true. But as soon as she'd seen
him tonight, she'd felt the old sparks leap between them.

She lowered her head into her hands, using her strong
will to banish his image from her consciousness. But it
refused to fade, and as she pictured him, the hairs on the
back of her neck stirred.

Danger. He was in danger. She felt it all the way to the
marrow of her bones.

"Wyatt!" Without considering her actions, she dashed
out of the tent and started running up the midway.

WYATT TURNED into the side lane the guy had told him
to take. Several paces along, he wondered if the barker
had steered him wrong. He was alone now, outside the
main traffic area of the carnival. A girl giggled, her high-
pitched voice flitting past him, and he felt the tap of fingers on his arm.

"Who's there?"

The only answer was another childish laugh. What was she doing out so late, all by herself?

Then her presence was gone, and he wondered if he'd dreamed her. He stopped worrying about the girl when he heard heavier footsteps dogging his path. Somebody was following him. Not a kid. A full-grown man, judging from the tread.

One thing he hadn't lost with his eyesight was his cop's instincts. Somebody was very purposefully trailing the blind man, probably with the intent of robbing him.

A dark bulky shape loomed to his right. A tent, he hoped, as he felt along the edge and detected coarse fabric. He was about to duck inside when he felt an arm catch him around the neck.

Acting instinctively, he dropped the cane, shot his elbow back into soft abdominal tissue.

As the mugger grunted, Wyatt went into a crouch, then flipped the assailant over his shoulders and heard him land heavily on the ground.

A curse sprang to the man's lips, a low and dangerous sound, as he climbed slowly to his feet, breathing hard.

Good, Wyatt had done some damage.

Staying limber, he waited for the attacker to make his move, hoping the blind man had the advantage of darkness.

There was a blur of sound, a rush of movement in the humid air. Wyatt ducked away, felt a heavy body hurtle past him at the same time that hot pain sliced along his ribs, and he knew he'd been cut. The bastard had a knife.

He crouched, making himself a smaller target, waiting for the next move—wishing he could see the man. The mugger was right-handed. He'd go for Wyatt's left side again.

All his concentration was on fending off the next attack

and getting in a solid blow of his own—until he heard running feet, heard a woman shouting. "Help! Somebody help!"

ALESSANDRA RUSHED DOWN the dark passageway between the tents—a back alley, used by the carnival folk, not the public. In the dim light she could see two men struggling on the ground. She couldn't see their faces, but she knew without doubt that one was Wyatt.

"Help!" she screamed again, this time in Romany, the language that everyone in the carnival knew and would respond to.

One of the men on the ground wrenched himself away and staggered off into the darkness.

She saw Wyatt sagging back against the side of a tent, heard his ragged breathing.

In response to her call, the narrow passage had filled with people.

"Get back. Give him air," Alessandra ordered. Then, "Oh, Lord, you're bleeding," she gasped as she saw the dark stain spreading across his shirt.

"I'm fine."

"Sure. Fine." As she tugged his shirt from the waistband of his slacks, she couldn't hold back a small sound of protest.

"How bad?" he asked.

"It's not deep. I can't see it very well. I need better light. Can you walk?"

"Of course," he replied, pushing himself to his feet, then swaying unsteadily.

She was instantly at his side, supporting his weight.

"He's an outsider. Send him to the emergency room," someone shouted.

"He was hurt in our camp. I'll take care of him," she

answered. The response was automatic. Wyatt was hurt and it was her fault. She had sent him away—into danger.

There were more arguments from her friends and relatives as she steered the injured man through the crowd.

She felt him struggle against her, knew he wanted to walk completely under his own power, but she kept him close.

Milo loomed in her path, blocking the way. "He doesn't belong here," he growled.

She raised defiant eyes to him. He owned the carnival. He could insist that Wyatt leave, but he stepped aside as she advanced.

The crowd thinned as she approached her trailer. Glancing at Wyatt, she saw that his eyes were squeezed tightly closed.

"We're here," she said, her voice low and soft.

"Where?"

"At my trailer." Her trailer. Her home. Like the caravans her people had once used. Only updated—with many of the modern conveniences Americans took for granted.

She'd never brought him here before. Never. Even though she'd known he'd wanted desperately to come inside and hold her in his arms, devour her with kisses.

Now she struggled to keep her voice steady as she said, "It's two steps up."

Inside, she led him down the short hall to her living area. She'd left an empty china teacup and saucer on the carved wooden table by the window. The newspaper on the floor, and a basket of laundry to be folded. Now she thought she should have cleaned up—until she remembered that he couldn't see the disorder.

Her daybed was on the far side of the room, opposite the love seat. She led him there.

"Where are you taking me?"

"My bed," she managed, her throat thick.

"I'll get blood on your spread."

"No, I've got a towel," she answered, grabbing one from the laundry basket and pressing it against his side. He was injured. No threat to her. Yet he seemed to fill the small room. Her room. Her personal space.

He reached down, felt the spread, stroking his fingers over the silky fabric.

"Lie down," she said, hearing the thickness in her own voice.

Awkwardly, he lowered himself to the horizontal surface, lying with his eyes closed and his hands pressed flat against the spread.

A man in her bed. Lord, he looked primal. Sexual.

Then she sternly reminded herself why he was here.

"I'll be right back," she murmured, and hurried to the tiny supply closet, where she got out antiseptic and bandages.

After filling a bowl with hot water, she eased down beside him. She rolled up his shirt and gently dabbed at the wound.

"How bad?"

"It's long but it's not deep," she said. "You must have dodged aside."

She cleaned the area, then spread on antiseptic. When he gasped, she went instantly still.

"What? What's wrong? Did I hurt you?"

"I...saw the wound," he said in a shaky voice.

"You imagined it? From my description?"

"I saw it!"

"But..."

"I'm blind. Seeing is impossible. Except for dark and light. But I saw. I think I saw what you were seeing. I think it's because you're touching me. It happened before, in your fortune-teller's tent. When you caught me and then again when you were holding my hand.''

She shook her head. What he was telling her was impossible. And yet, among her people, she'd heard of such things happening between a man and a woman who had formed a connection.

''No,'' she whispered, her gaze on the bright paisley shapes of the spread.

''Yellow and green swirly things,'' he said thickly. ''With some little designs of red and blue.''

She couldn't hold back a gasp. He'd never seen her home—her bed. Yet he'd just told her what the spread looked like. At least as a man might describe it.

Her gaze shot to his face. His eyes were closed again, but his breathing had quickened.

He didn't say any more about seeing through her eyes, didn't press the point, and she was grateful for that. Maybe it only happened when his eyes were open. He seemed to keep them closed much of the time. She was half-afraid to touch him now, but she forced herself to tape gauze over the wound.

He lay absolutely still while she tended to him.

''Thank you,'' he said when she had finished.

''You were hurt. I couldn't leave you hurt.''

''Anyone else out there would have.''

''No,'' she answered automatically, thinking that he probably spoke the truth. ''Why were you there?'' she asked. ''That wasn't a public area.''

''I was looking for a phone. Maybe I lost my way. Or maybe the barker near the entrance deliberately sent me down there.''

''Which barker?'' she asked quickly.

''The one at the ring toss. I can't give you much description. From his voice, I'd say he was in his twenties or thirties.''

"Tony. He's thirty-two," she said aloud. She was thinking Tony might have remembered Wyatt from before, and he might have wished him ill. Had Tony been the one who'd attacked him? She'd have to do some investigating.

"Don't get yourself into trouble because of me," he said sharply, giving her the eerie feeling that he'd read her mind.

"I won't," she answered, hoping he believed her. She didn't like the way his eyes narrowed, but when he spoke, it was to change the subject.

"Anyway, I'm lucky you came along. Lucky you interrupted before he fileted me."

Not luck, she thought. She had *known* he was in trouble. Yet she didn't mention that.

"Well, it's not deep," she said again, lamely.

"Yes." As he spoke, he reached up, his hand steady, and she thought he must be judging the distance by the sound of her voice. Slowly he clasped his palm around the back of her head and brought her mouth down toward his.

She could have resisted, should have resisted. But resistance was beyond her. Her lips touched down softly on his, the kiss sweet and at the same time edged with a passion she struggled to contain.

WYATT KNEW in some part of his mind that Alessandra had brought him into her home only because he was injured. But he was less aware of the wound than of the bed on which he lay.

Alessandra's bed.

It was all he could do to keep himself from pulling her

down to lie beside him so that he could show her just how much he had missed her.

She sighed his name, sighed the syllables into his mouth. And in that moment he knew she had missed him as much as he had missed her.

He lay there with his eyes closed. The hand that had clasped her head stroked over her back. The other palm stayed flat on the bed—lest he raise it to cup her breast.

He wanted to touch her—to engage all his remaining senses. He wanted to see her. She was touching him and he had seen before when she touched him. But only through her eyes. He wouldn't see her. So he kept his eyes closed, thinking he shouldn't be doing this at all. Yet he simply couldn't help himself.

A knock at the door made her bolt up and away from him as if they'd been doing something wrong—when nothing in the past two years had felt so right.

He heard the rustle of her clothing, felt her climb swiftly off the bed and dart down the short hallway. "Who is it?"

"Andrei," a gruff voice answered.

Ah, Andrei Sobatka. Another cousin. A handsome devil, a real ladies' man, if Wyatt remembered correctly. Doubtless he was coming to make sure that nothing funny was going on in here. Too late!

He heard the door open.

"I brought his cane."

"Thank you."

"We should call a cab and send him home. Sabina agrees with me. She says it's not proper to have him here. She says you must send him away."

Sabina. Her sister. Very similar in looks, as he recalled. He remembered her as seeming sad and defeated. Apparently she'd become more assertive. Like Alessandra.

"I'll take him home when he's better," Alessandra said.

"Don't you think you've done enough for him?"

"He was hurt by one of us."

"You don't know that! It could have been somebody from town planning to rob him."

He heard her wait a beat, wondering if she was going to mention Tony, the guy who had sent him astray. But all she said was, "He needs to rest." Her voice was firm. So was the sound of the door closing.

She stayed at the far end of the hallway, and bitter disappointment flooded through him. She had stood up for him, but what was he expecting now? That she'd take up where they'd left off? Sure. With a blind man. A blind man she hated because she thought his father had worked overtime to convict her cousin of murder. Still, when her lips had touched his, he hadn't felt hatred in her kiss. He had tasted sweetness, desire, a connection between them. And he wanted more.

He heard her slow footsteps returning and directed his nonexistent gaze to the spot where he thought she was standing. His mouth was suddenly dry, but he managed to get the words out that he'd planned.

"You're sure Carlo's innocent. Well, maybe I can help you prove it—one way or the other."

"How?"

Wyatt heard hope in her voice, also doubt. Maybe mistrust. He couldn't fault her for that.

"When my father retired he took some of his old files with him."

"Doesn't his work belong to the police department?" she shot back.

"Most of them, yes," he admitted. "But a cop can keep his own files on important cases. I certainly did. And there's no reason to believe Dad was any different.'' Quickly he added, ''If we can find the folder on Carlo's case, maybe we can turn up something you can use.''

''Why would you want to help me?'' she demanded. ''Why should I trust you? How do I know you won't just string me along—delaying the truth until it's too late for Carlo?''

Because I care about you. Because I never stopped. Those words stayed locked in his throat. He couldn't say them. It wouldn't be fair to her. It hadn't worked out the first time. Now he had nothing to offer her—besides the help he might be able to give her. Yet the need to cling to what time he had with her was overwhelming.

He heard himself saying, ''You should trust me because I sensed that my father is uneasy about his case. Maybe something wasn't done right. Maybe…'' He paused, brushed back his hair with his hand. ''I don't know. There was a lot of pressure to convict Carlo. Maybe…'' Again he stopped, unable to voice the unthinkable.

''How could you help?'' she asked, her voice softening.

''You mean how could a blind man help you?''

''That's not what I meant,'' she answered. By the tone of her voice, he was pretty sure that was what she'd been thinking. It was funny about being blind. There was a myth that blindness sharpened your other senses. It wasn't true, of course. But it made you use what you had more carefully. Hearing. Smell. Touch. Even taste.

He listened to what people said very carefully now. Not just their words.

Sighing, he answered the spoken question. ''I was a damn good police detective. Now I work with the police in several jurisdictions, on old cases that nobody else has the time for. I go over the paperwork, the evidence. Sometimes I have an assistant to help search through the files.

I also use a scanner that reads material to me. When the reports are already on the computer, I convert them to voice. I also reinterview witnesses, try to pick up things the initial investigators missed. You'd be surprised how much you can learn from tone of voice, for example. From evasive answers. I've closed some old cases the cops had given up on.''

"You'd help find out the truth about Carlo?'' she breathed, and this time he heard hope in her voice.

"I'd do it for you.'' He swallowed, thinking he might as well make this as convincing as he could. "When you sent me away before, you did it because I was Louis Boudreaux's son. I want you to know that my father isn't a bad man. That he was doing his job the best he could.'' He might have added that he had another motive, too. He'd be close to Alessandra—for as long as the investigation took.

"So you think Carlo's guilty?'' she asked, some of the color going from her tone.

"He was convicted. That was good enough for the State of Louisiana. But I won't presume his guilt or innocence now. I'll do my best to find out the truth.''

"Okay.''

He held out his hand. "We should shake on it.''

For a heartbeat she didn't move. He strained his ears, waiting. When she finally crossed the carpeted floor, he let the breath ease out of his lungs.

Her hand met his, and he closed his fingers around hers, held tight for several seconds, feeling the same kind of connection he'd felt when they'd kissed. Perhaps he was a coward, but he kept his eyes closed because he was afraid to see his own strained face.

He felt her fingers tremble. Then she pulled her hand

back. "Andrei knocked on the door to make a point. I have to go talk to my family about your being here."

"Before somebody thinks you're doing more than dressing my cut?"

"Our community is like a small town," she answered. "We've been together for a long time, and people know other people's business. They'll talk, no matter what happens."

"Then tell them I'm going to help you investigate Carlo's case."

"They may not believe me."

"Let's hope you're wrong."

"Why?" she asked sharply.

"Because you may not have mentioned it to Andrei, but you and I both know that barker didn't wish me well. For all I know, he sent my cab away so he could ambush me. Maybe he was just having some fun. Maybe it was more than that."

"No," she answered automatically, but her voice lacked conviction. Then, "You need to rest. And I need to go and talk to my family. They're in my sister's trailer. Valonia's there."

"Carlo's mother?"

"Yes."

"She should be delighted to hear you're consorting with me."

In the silence that followed, he knew he should find some way to get home. But he also knew from experience that the cab company had shut down for the night. And if he asked one of her relatives, he'd probably end up with a knife sticking between his ribs, not just trailing across them. Actually, he could manufacture lots of excuses for staying here, even when he knew she was putting herself in a compromising position. For him.

But he was needy tonight. Too needy for chivalry. He'd accept the offer to sleep in Alessandra's bed, on her perfumed sheets and pillows, because that might be as close to her as he would ever get.

So instead of offering to clear out, he said, "If you're going to leave me alone, I need to know the layout of this room." He swallowed, hating to admit weakness. "Otherwise, I'll feel trapped here."

"Yes. I understand."

She moved toward him again, and he knew by where her voice came from next that she'd hunkered down on the floor beside the bed, her face inches from his.

"My trailer is about ten feet wide and fourteen feet long. The bed is in the corner farthest from the door. The couch is opposite you. There's a chair and a table against the wall between them. The hall between us and the kitchen is lined with closets. The exit door is to your right, just before the kitchen. The bathroom is a rectangle opposite the front door. It's small. A toilet, a sink, a shower. There are shelves above the toilet."

"Let me make sure I have all that straight," he said. "I'll need my cane."

"I'd better get a few things out of the way first." He heard her scurrying around the room, heard a cup rattling in a saucer and newspaper rustling. A woman straightening up her house for company—even when the company couldn't see the disorder.

She hurried down the hall to the kitchen, and the cup and saucer clanked into a stainless-steel sink. Then she was back.

Pushing himself up, he was annoyed to find that his footing wasn't quite as sure as he would have liked. Alessandra was instantly at his side. Eyes closed, he clasped her slender waist, simply because the contact felt good.

But pride had him asking for the cane so he could move around on his own.

She put the white staff into his hand, and he used it to locate the furniture and the features that she'd mentioned.

"Okay. I can find my way around," he said, standing by the door.

"You'll be all right?"

"Fine."

She hesitated. "I never lock the door. We trust each other here, but I'm going to lock it now. You can open it from the inside if you need to.

"Thanks."

OUT IN THE DARKNESS through the open window, some-one had been listening with great interest to the private conversation between Wyatt and Alessandra. Now it was time to move to a different location.

Quickly the black-clad figure glided to the side of a nearby trailer, then faded back into the shadows as Alessandra's door opened.

She stepped out, her features illuminated by one of the lights that had been set up in the area where the carnies camped.

Well, not camped, exactly. Each family or individual had a traveling home—some of them quite comfortable. Like Alessandra's little nest with its rich wall hangings, fringed pillows and thick rugs.

Wyatt Boudreaux was standing just inside the door, and she turned to say something the watcher couldn't catch. Not from here.

Then she closed the door and hurried more deeply into the family compound—leaving the blind man inside.

Yes, Wyatt Boudreaux was blind. But he was still the enemy, still dangerous. He should have been warned off this evening. Instead, he'd offered to help Alessandra save her cousin, and she'd accepted. They were going to try to unearth information that was better off buried.

Like the woman Carlo was supposed to have murdered, Theresa Granville. She'd been dead for ten years. Carlo would be dead in another few weeks.

The killing should end there. But it wouldn't, because Wyatt Boudreaux had changed the rules. He'd gotten involved, and taken Alessandra with him. Too bad for her.

The watcher's face contorted. Now both of them would have to die. And soon—before they unearthed any inconvenient evidence.

Chapter Three

Alessandra knocked on Sabina's door.

"Come in," her sister called.

When she made her way down the hall, she found the room already crowded with people. Andrei was there. And Valonia. From the looks on their faces, she knew they'd been discussing her. Sinking to the nest of pillows near the doorway, she sat with her skirt tucked under her and her arms clasped around her knees.

Valonia gave her a narrow-eyed look. As Wyatt had mentioned, she was Carlo's mother. What he didn't know was that the older woman had been like a mother to Alessandra and her sister for the past fifteen years, after their own parents had died in an accident trying to make it to the next town when the roads in the low-lying bayou country were flooded.

"Wyatt Boudreaux is still in your trailer?" Sabina asked, her voice mild but her green eyes flashing.

"As I told Andrei, he was hurt tonight because of us. And before you try to contradict me, maybe you'd better ask Tony why he sent Wyatt down that passageway between the tents."

"Tony sent him there?" Sabina echoed.

"Yes. Deliberately. When he asked directions to a telephone. We're camped right beside the bayou. If he'd kept walking down that lane between the tents, he would have ended up in the water—maybe in an alligator's jaws.''

Andrei made a dismissive sound. ''Tony must have recognized him as Boudreaux's son. Remember, he and Carlo were best friends.''

''So did Tony attack him with a knife?'' Alessandra asked.

''Tony wouldn't do anything like that.''

''Well, he's your best friend, now, so of course you'd say that. But are you really sure?''

When Andrei looked down at his hands, she knew she'd made her point.

''Wyatt's not the enemy,'' she continued. ''He says he's going to look into Carlo's case—see if there's any hope of saving him.''

She saw Valonia's wrinkled face contort. She was old before her time. She'd aged ten years when her son had been arrested, ten more when he'd been convicted. Carlo's troubles had changed her, made her bitter and unable to trust any *gadje*. ''He's lying,'' she said now. ''He's his father's son. He wants Carlo to die.''

Alessandra shook her head. ''No. He came here with doubts. What could it hurt to let him try and help us?''

''He could be pretending to help,'' Valonia answered, her voice rising. ''What if he's just stalling until it's too late for Carlo?''

Alessandra had had that thought herself. Now she said, ''Then we won't be any worse off than we are now.''

Valonia's dark eyes were fierce. ''That's easy for you to say. Carlo's not your son.''

Alessandra scrambled up and went to her, kneeling beside the older woman and throwing her arms around her.

"Oh, Little Mother, I know how Carlo's punishment hurts you."

"No, you don't. Not until you have a child of your own. And if you're thinking that you would have that child with Wyatt Boudreaux, then you are betraying me, betraying your heritage, betraying yourself."

Alessandra felt as though the old woman had slapped her in the face. She was floundering for an answer when there was a sharp rap at the door.

Without waiting to be invited, Milo Vasilli strode into the room, followed by his daughter, Florica.

The carnival owner was a square-built man with graying hair and dark eyes. Florica, a woman in her mid-twenties, had his sharp features, but there was a childlike quality about her that made her seem much younger.

Milo reached into his pocket and pulled out the gold coin he always carried, flipping it in the air as he said, "You're consorting with that Wyatt Boudreaux."

The accusation made Florica giggle, the way she often did at inappropriate times. Ignoring her, Alessandra raised her head toward Milo. "I'm not consorting with him. He's agreed to help us reopen Carlo's case."

"And you believe him?"

"That's what I just asked her!" Valonia said.

Alessandra stood, looking at the accusing faces around the room. "None of you will give him a chance."

"That's right. I won't. I have the final say here, and I want him out of here," Milo said. "Now."

"He can't leave tonight. We can talk about this in the morning—when we're all a little calmer."

Without waiting for a reply, she turned, brushed past Milo and his daughter, and headed for the door.

"Alessandra, wait," Sabina called. But Alessandra ignored the plea in her sister's voice.

Out in the damp night air, she stood breathing hard. Was she a fool for trusting Wyatt? For trusting a *gadjo?*

Maybe. Maybe she'd let herself get carried away by emotions she had no business feeling.

Through the wall behind her, she could hear a babble of voices. They were talking about her again. Well, she'd deal with them in the morning. And deal with Wyatt. Maybe the best thing *was* to send him home. But then they'd never see his father's old files.

She pressed the palms of her hands against her eyes. She had the ability to see the future—sometimes. But not her own future. Never her own.

Usually she understood why that was a blessing. But at times like this, she thought it was a curse.

A low sound escaped from her throat. She was confused. And tired. Worn-out, physically and emotionally. Any decisions were best made in the light of day.

WYATT TENSED when he heard the key in the lock. It was probably Alessandra, although he wasn't going to assume that.

After she'd left, he'd walked around her trailer, getting comfortable with the layout and turning off lights so he'd only be a shadow in the darkness. Next he'd used the bathroom so he wouldn't be fumbling around in there while she was home. And finally he'd made his way to her kitchen and taken a good, sharp knife from the drawer. He held it against his side now, waiting in the darkness.

The footsteps that crossed the room were soft and light. A woman. Alessandra, surely. Unless the man who'd attacked him had sent a female accomplice to finish the job.

He lay unmoving, waiting. She said nothing. He sensed her standing over him, probably looking down. He might have reached up and found her hand, but he sensed more.

She didn't speak, and he was pretty sure that the meeting with her family hadn't gone well.

Judging from Andrei's reaction earlier, they'd probably urged her to throw him out on his ear.

Long moments passed. At last she sighed and recrossed the room. He heard rustling sounds, heard her go into the bathroom. Then she padded softly across the room again and settled on the love seat.

He should be the one on the love seat rather than the bed, he thought. But he didn't want to give away the fact that he was awake by suggesting it. Instead, he lay there listening to the sound of her breathing. It had been a long time since he'd shared that sort of intimacy with a woman. He liked the sound, liked it when the rhythm changed, indicating sleep, because it meant she felt comfortable enough to relax with him here.

He needed to sleep, as well. Tomorrow was going to be difficult. Closing his eyes, he focused on the mental exercises that helped him relax. In minutes he had joined Alessandra in slumber.

HE WOKE UP choking, gasping, his lungs burning and heat beating at his back—and knew at once that the trailer was on fire.

"Alessandra!" He called her name, but it came out as a choked gasp. "Alessandra."

Across the room, he could hear her coughing. He pushed himself off the bed, tried to stand and almost strangled. The smoke was thicker near the ceiling.

Dropping to the floor, he crawled across the trailer toward the love seat. When he got there, he called her name again.

He heard her gasping for breath.

"Stay...down," he ordered, unable to waste more breath.

The room was full of smoke and heat. And he imagined tall shapes flickering around him. Flames? Could he see flames with his minimal ability to sense dark and light?

He didn't know. His brain felt foggy, and his lungs burned with every breath. He wanted to pick her up and carry her from the room. But he didn't think he had the strength. More than that, he knew that standing would only put his head into the smoke again.

So he dragged her off the couch.

"I...which way..."

Realizing she was totally disoriented in the smoke and darkness, he led her across the room, staying low. They made it to the hallway where the air was a little less smoky, and he gave a silent prayer of thanks. Trying to keep his breath shallow, he moved toward the door, still leading Alessandra, his eyes squeezed shut against the smoke.

Outside he could hear somebody shouting, "Fire!" Then more voices joined in.

He had reached the door when he heard the lock jiggling followed by somebody cursing.

"I can't get in! She locked the door!" a man shouted.

"Get an ax. Somebody get an ax. They're going to burn up in there!"

Chapter Four

Wyatt felt as if his brain were filling with smoke. Raising his hand, he fumbled with the lock. When it clicked, he twisted the knob, then threw his weight against the door.

It flew open, and he spilled out into blessed oxygen-filled air, taking Alessandra with him. He was falling, and he remembered that he'd climbed a couple of steps when he'd entered the trailer.

He would have hit the ground hard, but hands caught him and eased him down.

Activity swirled around him as he lay there panting, the cool air like springtime in his lungs. Someone grabbed his shoulders, helped him move away from the trailer.

He heard a gurgling sound. Water through a large hose. Some of it splashed his feet and legs.

"Alessandra? Where's Alessandra? Is she all right?" he croaked.

Near him he heard coughing. "I'm…here. I'm all right."

"Thank God." He turned toward her, reached for her and felt her hand clamp onto his.

He held tight, relieved by the strength of her grip since it meant she couldn't be injured too badly.

"I got all turned around. I wouldn't have gotten out of there without you," she gasped.

"It's okay. We're both okay," was all he could manage. He kept his hold on her, listening to the babble of voices around him. If he opened his eyes, would he be able to see? He tried it and found that the shared vision trick wasn't working. The first time it had shocked him. The second time had been deliberate. But apparently he couldn't count on it working all the time. And in this case, he was grateful, because he really didn't want to see a ring of hostile faces.

A woman was speaking, and Alessandra called her Sabina. The sister.

"What happened?" Sabina asked.

"Somebody set the trailer on fire," Wyatt said.

"Who would do that?" a man demanded.

He recognized the voice from earlier. It was the cousin, Andrei.

"Maybe the same guy who knifed me," Wyatt said. His mind was racing now. "Somebody who wanted to kill me—and Alessandra, too."

"No!" the sister protested.

"Okay, what's your explanation?"

Nobody answered. He heard another woman talking to Alessandra, asking questions in a low voice. Then he caught the distant wail of sirens. The fire department. And an ambulance.

"Tell me what's going on," he demanded.

"The trailer is smoldering. I think the fire is out."

Unconsciously, his hold tightened on Alessandra's hand. If she broke the contact, he'd be lost in the sea of people around him. People who hated his guts.

She must have sensed what he was feeling because she held tight to him and inched closer. She only let go when the paramedics separated them. An efficient team worked over him, assessing his injuries, which he kept assuring them were minimal.

Then he and Alessandra were loaded into an ambulance for a ride to the emergency room. Two hours later, they were both pronounced fit to leave. And they'd been interviewed by the local cops.

He knew her relatives were out in the waiting room, eager to take her home. Before they came through the door, he turned to her.

"I don't want you going back there tonight."

"But—"

"Somebody tried to kill both of us." He sucked in a breath and let it out. "I don't know much about your people. Would they turn on a woman who had taken up with a...*gadjo?*"

A LITTLE RIPPLE of shock went through Alessandra. "You know that word?" she asked carefully.

"Yes," he said, making a dismissive gesture with his hand. "Remember, I'm a...I was a cop. I do my research. In your language, Romany, the word for a male outsider is *gadjo.* The word's a symbol of hostility to outsiders."

"No," she shot back. "It's a symbol of the world's hostility to us."

He sighed. "Okay. That's fair. But there's no point in arguing about who did what to whom. The important question is, would some of your people turn against you for taking me in?"

"No," she answered immediately, but unlike her previous response, there was no strength behind the denial.

"So there might be fanatics who would try to make an example of you?"

"I can't believe one of my people would hurt me."

"Well, somebody set that fire. But there could be an- other explanation. It could be somebody who thinks we can find out who really murdered Theresa Granville."

"What are you saying?" she asked.

"That the real murderer was listening to us talking to- night—and got worried."

"Then you think Carlo didn't do it?" she asked, hope leaping in her breast.

"It's a logical explanation. We need to go over my father's papers as soon as possible. I want you to come home with me—away from the carnival."

She looked down at her hands, knowing that by all logic, she should refuse. But logic wasn't ruling her now. When she realized that Wyatt couldn't see her warring emotions, she lifted her head.

His face was etched with tension as he said, "You could help me with the papers. First thing in the morning. The sooner we get started, the sooner we may find some- thing." He expelled a long breath. "We can get the cops to give us a ride home."

"I think Andrei is still waiting for me."

"Tell him you've made other arrangements."

"You sound like you don't trust him."

"He didn't want me staying in your trailer," Wyatt pointed out.

"But he would never hurt me. You've got to believe that. We've been close since we were little. We grew up together. He's always protected me and Sabina."

Wyatt nodded. "Okay, I'll accept your judgment. And—" he coughed "—there are other advantages to be- ing a police officer wounded in the line of duty. I won't have any trouble getting the local cops to keep my house under surveillance."

"You think that's necessary?"

"Yes. If someone can torch your trailer, they can do the same to my house."

"You think it was deliberate?"

"If not, it was a hell of a coincidence."

As she sucked in a sharp breath, he continued, "So now that that's settled, we can make arrangements to leave."

She cleared her throat. "Uh, would you mind if I ask Andrei to bring you some clothes? Yours are…uh…" She hesitated again. "They're covered with dirt and soot."

He looked embarrassed, and she realized he hadn't thought at all about his appearance.

"We're both a mess," she added quickly. "I'll ask Sabina to bring me something, too."

"Why would Andrei do that for me?" he questioned.

"Because I asked him!"

"Sure. Fine," he answered.

But once she'd introduced the idea, he went a step further, and she found out there were still more advantages to being a decorated ex-cop who'd been wounded in the line of duty. People were willing to do him favors.

When he asked if both he and Alessandra could take a shower before leaving the hospital, they were allowed to use the staff facilities. An hour later, they were both washed and dressed in clean clothing and riding in the back of a patrol car.

He was wearing navy slacks and a blue button-down shirt that probably belonged to Andrei. She was wearing one of her sister's dresses—one that she'd admired in the past, actually.

She knew the emerald green and deep blue were perfect for her coloring. Then she remembered that wouldn't mean much to Wyatt—unless she gave him a description, and she wasn't willing to go that far.

As they rode to his house in the back of a black-and-white cruiser, she sat uneasily beside him, listening to him conferring with the uniformed officer who was driving.

"We don't have the manpower for plainclothes surveillance of your house twenty-four/seven. But there will be someone outside for the next few hours. Then off and on until this is over."

"Appreciate it," Wyatt answered as they pulled up in front of a white Victorian with a wide front porch and a turret at the right front corner. It was four in the morning, but there was a streetlight directly out front, and as they came up the brick walk, floodlights snapped on.

Wyatt might be blind, but he hadn't neglected the appearance of the house. The paint was fresh and the gardens well tended, the flower beds filled with begonias and other plants she couldn't name.

Alessandra couldn't suppress the feeling of envy that had bedeviled her over the years. People like Wyatt lived in big, comfortable houses surrounded by nice gardens; they put down roots. She and her family lived in tiny trailers and moved from place to place.

She knew that some of her family would not be capable of living in one place for long. Traveling was in their blood. But she could easily imagine living in a house like this—planting flowers and tending them. Transferring the decorating skills she'd used in her tiny home to a much larger canvas.

Then, as Wyatt ushered her into a square front hall, it struck her that she no longer had even her little refuge. It had been set on fire—perhaps by someone she had trusted all her life. And anything that hadn't been totally destroyed would be permeated with smoke.

She must have made a sound of distress, because he turned quickly toward her, his voice urgent. "What's wrong? Do you see something?"

"No…no…it's nothing to do with your house," she stammered, silently acknowledging that she wasn't telling the entire truth. "I just realized that all my things will be fire-damaged—or covered with soot."

"It's all my fault," he muttered.

She reached out and gripped his shoulders. "No!"

"If I hadn't come snooping around the carnival, it wouldn't have happened."

"Don't put the blame on yourself. You said before that it's because we're going to help Carlo."

There was a long moment of silence before he finally said, "I didn't put it quite that way."

"I know it didn't start out like that for you. But now that someone's come after us…we have to find out who, not just for Carlo."

He sighed, looking weary. "Yeah."

She was instantly contrite. "I'm putting a lot on you."

"No more than I'm putting on myself. The only way we can guarantee our safety is to figure out what someone wants to keep us from finding out."

"I…I talked to Andrei about Tony," she said. "Tony's sorry about sending you down that lane."

"He wanted to get back at Louis Boudreaux's son. I understand that."

"But he didn't attack you."

"How can you be sure?"

"I've known him all his life. He's a good man."

"You know all the people out there. *Somebody* hasn't lived up to your expectations."

She had no answer for him. Without switching on a lamp, he strode into a sitting room and stood with his back toward her. She followed him into the shadowy room, letting her eyes adjust to the dim light from the street filtering through the window. She couldn't see details—just a comfortable-looking couch and chairs. Polished wooden tables. A thick Oriental rug. Everything was scrupulously neat. Not like most men would keep their personal space. But necessary for a man who might trip over things left out of place.

He turned toward her, cleared his throat. "I wanted you to come here where you'd be safe. We can't do anything constructive tonight. We both need some sleep. There's a guest room upstairs. I'll show you where it is, and where I keep the clean towels."

She ignored the housekeeping information and asked, "Does the cut on your ribs hurt?"

"Not bad. We both know I could have gone home tonight."

"Thank God you didn't, or I'd be dead."

This time he was the one who protested the obvious. "No!"

In the shadowy room, she reached out and touched his arm, feeling his muscles jump under her fingers. "I didn't get around to thanking you for saving my life. You risked your own by dragging me outside."

"I wouldn't have left you in there," he said, his voice rough.

"I know." She closed the space between them, reaching out and clasping his shoulders.

He made a strangled sound and folded her close. The intensity with which he clung to her took her breath away.

It was so natural, so right to lift her head and find his lips with hers.

He had kissed her hours before, and that kiss had told her something about herself—and about him. They might have parted in anger five years ago, but they both still cared—deeply. Now there was more—passion flaring between them like heat lightning.

He tasted like the rich wine her people kept for special celebrations. Births and marriages. And at the same time, like all the things she'd told herself a woman of her people could never have.

When he lifted his head, they were both struggling to drag air into their lungs. Hours before they'd been struggling for breath in the fire. Now passion robbed them of oxygen.

"Don't," he said in a thick voice, taking a step back. But he kept his hand on her shoulder, as though he couldn't bear to let her go.

That was a good sign, she told herself. She'd found out tonight that this man possessed strength she had never suspected. She understood beyond a doubt that he would send her to his guest bedroom if she didn't let him know what she was feeling now.

She was a fortune-teller, a woman whose gift was spinning out the stories of other people's lives in beautiful, evocative language.

In this unfamiliar house, she could barely find the words she needed to speak, although she knew she must.

Chapter Five

Alessandra knew he couldn't see her face even if his eyes had been open, so she struggled to put what she was feeling into her voice. "Wyatt, you said you could have gone home tonight after you were cut. I didn't want you to go home. I wanted to keep you close."

"Maybe you saw the future—the fire," he said, his fingers clenching her shoulder.

Either he misunderstood her or he was deliberately trying to make less of what they both felt.

"No, I can never see my own future. It wasn't any sort of precognition that worked on me tonight. It was the past. I kept thinking about what happened five years ago."

"You sent me away," he reminded her.

"Yes, but I never stopped wanting you. Never. Even when I tried to tell myself I hated you for being Louis Boudreaux's son. But I'm not going to walk away from you tonight. Not when we're alone in this house—both wanting the same thing."

As she spoke, she reached up and covered his hand, pressing her fingers against his.

"I should go get that cop outside to come in and chaperon us," he growled.

"But you won't. Because this is our second chance."

"For what?"

"Wyatt Boudreaux, you're an intelligent man. Don't play dumb with me." More confident now, she moved closer, so close she could feel the heat coming off him—and the need.

This time when she kissed him, a sound welled from deep in his chest, a sound that told her he'd tried and failed to let her go.

"Alessandra." His warm breath fanned her as he spoke. Then his mouth was moving over hers again with an urgency that sent shock waves through her.

She needed to anchor herself to something solid—and Wyatt, with his wide, strong back, was her natural choice.

Her eyes drifted closed as she absorbed the impact of this man who had filled her thoughts on so many lonely nights. Seeking his warmth and strength, she pulled out the tails of his shirt, then slipped her hands underneath, stroking her fingers upward against his heated skin.

But that wasn't nearly enough. "Touch me," she murmured. "I need you to touch me." As she spoke, she brought his hands to the row of buttons down the front of her dress.

Still with his eyes closed, he worked by touch. With fingers that weren't entirely steady, he began to open the buttons. And her grasp was just as shaky as she helped him, their hands tangling as they met over her breasts.

"Lord, you're not wearing a bra," he breathed as he cupped her quivering flesh.

"Sabina forgot to bring me one." She gave a strangled laugh. "I think we're both happy about that."

The laughter ended in a choked exclamation as he found her hardened nipples, first with his fingers and then with his lips.

When she could speak again, she said, "Maybe we'd better find your bedroom."

"Up the stairs. The first room on the right."

He slung his arm around her waist as they started for the stairs, and the journey took longer than necessary, because they kept stopping to kiss and caress and to remove articles of clothing. By the time they reached the second floor, her dress and sandals had been discarded, along with his shirt and shoes.

In the bedroom, he turned and pulled her fully against him, and the feel of his hair-matted chest against her breasts made her knees buckle.

She sat down abruptly on the bed. He was still standing, and she pulled him close so that she could skim his slacks down his legs. Apparently his borrowed outfit hadn't included underwear, either.

His body was all taut muscle and magnificent arousal. With a low moan, she pressed her cheek and then her open mouth against his abdomen, feeling his muscles ripple under the intimate touch.

Then he was beside her on the bed, his hands stroking up and down her sides, sliding over her ribs, her hips, her thighs, then gathering her close.

His eyes were still tightly shut as he learned her body with his fingertips and his lips. And as he caressed her, he told her how much he had missed her, how much he wanted her, the hot, sexy words fueling her need.

Joyfully, she cradled his head against her breasts as his lips found one taut nipple and sucked it. The sensations were almost too exquisite to bear.

As she ran her hands down his back and over his taut buttocks, his fingers found the slick, hot core of her, and his knowing touch drove her wild.

"Wyatt...I need you now," she gasped. "Please, now."

He rose over her, claiming her, and for a breathless moment they both went very still as they absorbed the reality of their joining. Then he began to move with slow, gliding strokes that quickly became more urgent, more demanding. Gladness surged through her as she matched his rhythm.

His hand slid between them, stroking and pressing, and she was lost in a tight spiral of pleasure that built toward a burst of ecstasy. Crying out, she clung to the slick skin of his shoulders.

He was there with her all the way, his own glad cry mingling with hers as they held each other in the midst of the storm.

He shifted his weight off her, but she kept her fingers knit with his as he lay back against the sheets.

"Thank you," she breathed. "That was beautiful."

His fingers tightened on hers, but he said nothing, and she turned her head, seeing that his eyes were squeezed closed as though he were trying to shut out pain.

"You don't agree?" she whispered.

He didn't answer at once, and she died a little inside. Then he heaved a sigh. "Alessandra, I'm a blind ex-cop who lives in Les Baux on his pension and works cold cases to make himself feel useful. You're a fortune-teller with a carnival. When the midway packs up and moves, you'll go with your family."

"No!"

They weren't touching now, but he turned his head toward her, his eyes wide open for the first time since they'd arrived at his house, and she felt as if he were looking into her soul. "Which part did I get wrong?"

"You don't have to put it in those terms."

"I'm trying to be realistic."

"You're trying to make me feel like making love with you was a mistake—when I know it wasn't."

"You may see things differently in the morning."

"Wyatt, please…don't…" Maybe he was right. But she wasn't going to admit that now. And if he *was* right, if they indeed had no future together, then she was going to grab every scrap of happiness she could. Rolling toward him, she pressed her lips to his and gloried in the response that he wasn't able to hide.

ALESSANDRA SENSED it was still early when she woke up alone in the double bed. The night before, she had seen the room only in shadow. Now she sat up and stared around. The furniture was charming—old, polished oak pieces that had either been in this house for years or that he'd purchased at antique shops. There was no rug, only a wide-planked wooden floor.

She was about to climb out of bed when she heard footsteps. Automatically, she snatched the covers over her breasts, then went very still as Wyatt stepped into the room.

He was naked. His dark hair was damp, and it was obvious he'd just showered and shaved.

"You're awake," he said without looking in her direction as he crossed to the dresser and opened a drawer. She saw him take out a pair of briefs and step into them. "After breakfast we can start looking around my father's office—at the stuff I told you he brought home."

She watched him pull on a navy polo shirt and jeans, only half listening to what he was saying. She'd come here to look at his father's papers. But she found herself focusing on the man who had made passionate love to her the night before. He was so handsome, and so sure of his movements here in his own home that you wouldn't know he was blind. Yet blindness had changed his whole life—in ways she couldn't imagine. He'd tried to tell her that last night. She hadn't wanted to listen. But she knew she would have to deal with it, because it was what he dealt with every day.

"He was very meticulous. He wrote up notes for himself. And maybe he'll be willing to talk to you about Carlo when I tell him I think someone tried to kill us to keep us from digging into the case now."

She forced her voice to work. "Where is he?"

"In a nursing home not far from here. He had a stroke last year. So you may have trouble understanding his speech. It's a bit slurred."

"I'm sorry."

"It's been rough for him."

Alessandra saw the pain that stiffened his features. There had been times when she'd cursed Louis Boudreaux. When she'd wished that something terrible would happen to the man. It seemed that she'd gotten her wish, but it didn't give her the feeling of satisfaction she'd imagined.

"I'll fix breakfast while you're getting dressed," Wyatt said, his tone and his expression smoothing out.

"All right. " Telling herself that he couldn't see her anyway, she climbed out of bed, then snatched up the dress Wyatt had apparently retrieved from the stairs. Holding it in front of herself, she grabbed the bag Sabina had packed for her.

When she brushed past Wyatt, he stopped her with a hand on her bare shoulder.

"Wait!"

"I'm embarrassed to be standing here naked," she murmured.

"I know that." She saw him swallow. "I just wanted to say what I should have said last night. Making love with you was…the best thing that's happened to me in a long time."

"Thank you for…sharing that with me," she murmured.

"I never was much good at expressing my feelings," he went on, "and it hasn't gotten any easier in the past few years. I mean, if you'd lost something important, if you'd suddenly found you couldn't tell people's fortunes, you might have some trouble with your self-image."

She put aside her own embarrassment and turned to embrace him, knowing that what he'd said had taken guts.

He clasped her to him, his hands traveling up and down the length of her back. "I can't make myself believe there's any way we can stay together," he said.

"Maybe if we want it enough, we can make it work," she answered, praying it was possible.

He nodded tightly, and she knew he couldn't let himself believe there was any hope for the two of them. Partly it was her fault. She'd used the harshest possible terms when she'd sent him away five years ago. That was bad enough to overcome. His being blinded had made their chances much worse. Not because she thought any less of him. Actually, just the reverse was true. She was astounded by how well he'd adapted. But she knew his altered self-image might not let him reach out for happiness.

And then there was the problem of Carlo. What if they couldn't find something that would prevent his execution? Then she and Wyatt would be right back where they'd started. On opposite sides of an earthquake fault.

She voiced none of those thoughts but simply said, "I'd better get dressed."

"Yes." His hands fell away from her, and she made a speedy exit from the room.

Down the hall, she took a quick shower, brushed her teeth, then decided that she might as well put on last night's dress, since she hadn't worn it very long. Then she'd call Milo. She needed to find out about her trailer, and maybe the carnival owner would be willing to give her a few days off. Sabina could fill in for her. Or even Valonia.

Thinking of the old woman gave her a little chill. She and Valonia were close. Yet there were people who never understood why. There was something dark and secretive about the woman. A strange component to her personality that put people off unless they got close to her. It was even whispered that she had the ability to curse the lives of her enemies.

Louis Boudreaux had been one of those enemies. Maybe that was equally true of Wyatt. What would Valonia do if her niece and the man whose father had helped convict Carlo got back together? Was that dangerous for Wyatt? Would fear for his welfare be the reason she would have to walk away from him?

A shiver traveled over her skin and sank into her flesh, all the way to her bones. She clenched her teeth, but couldn't hold back a low, frightened sound.

Something bad was going to happen. She didn't know what it was, but she knew it was coming. Maybe it had to do with Valonia. Maybe not. But Alessandra had learned to believe in the flashes of precognition that came to her at random times. And learned to dread them.

WYATT SET UP the electric pot to brew Kona coffee, then opened the refrigerator and took out Cajun sausage and a carton of eggs. Might as well impress Alessandra with his cooking skills.

Working by feel, on a cutting board with a rim, he sliced some sausage, along with onions and peppers, then put them in the skillet with olive oil. The heat control had special markings so that he could tell the temperature.

When he'd first been blinded, he'd sunk into despair. Then he'd vowed to do almost everything he'd done before. There were frustrations, of course. Like having to rely on cabdrivers like Henry Beaver. Thinking of Henry made him wonder what had happened to him last night. From memory, he dialed the cab company and asked for last night's driver.

Henry happened to be in the office.

"You need a ride somewhere?" he asked.

"No. But I want to ask you about the carnival. Why did you leave when I asked you to wait for me?"

"You told this guy that I didn't have to. That you wouldn't be needing me."

"Who was this guy?"

"Some guy leaving the midway with his kids. Said somebody'd told him to speak to the cabdriver waiting at the entrance and tell him he could leave."

Wyatt felt a surge of anger, but there was no point in taking out his frustration on Henry. "I guess somebody was playing a prank on us. Next time, wait until you hear from me directly, okay?"

"Got it."

Hanging up, Wyatt stood thinking about the incident. Then the aroma of the heating sausage reminded him he'd better pay attention to what he was cooking.

Still, his mind kept working as he tested a piece of onion with a fork. Dad had sent him to the carnival last night to get information, and he should report back. But he was strangely reluctant to make the call. He hadn't told Henry that leaving him stranded had almost gotten him killed. And he was even more reluctant to tell his father about the murder attempt. That would only upset the old man. In addition, he didn't want to talk about his relationship with Alessandra King, Carlo Mustov's cousin.

He knew his father wouldn't approve—or be thrilled at all by his offer to help Alessandra save her cousin.

His features were pensive as he cracked eggs into a small bowl and added salt and pepper before scrambling them. He'd always admired his father. In fact, his dad was one of the reasons he'd gone to the police academy. But now, when he thought about Carlo Mustov, he got a bad feeling in the pit of his stomach.

He'd just finished pouring the eggs into the pan when he heard Alessandra on the stairs and quickly rearranged his features.

She stopped in the kitchen doorway. "I was going to offer to help, but I see you've got it pretty well finished."

"You can set the table and pour coffee. There's milk in the refrigerator if you want it, and the sugar bowl is on the counter by the coffeepot. The cutlery is in the drawer beside the refrigerator."

"Everything's very efficient."

"It has to be." He sprinkled cheese over the eggs, then put a top on the pan, listening to the clink of knives and forks on the table. The sound made him think about how solitary his existence had been since his dad had gone into the nursing home.

"Can I use your phone after breakfast to call Milo?" she asked.

"Of course. Feel free to use anything you want. Do you drive?"

"Yes."

"Well, Dad's car is in the garage. I've had the service station keep it in good running order, because I was planning to sell it. Now you might as well get some use out of it."

"I can drive out to the carnival."

"No!" The command came out low and sharp, taking them both by surprise.

"Why not?" she asked, a sudden quaver in her voice.

He filled his lungs, then let the air out in an even stream. "Because you're in danger out there."

"I live there."

"Let's not forget about the fire somebody set."

He heard her breath catch. "I can't hide out here forever."

"How about until we catch the person who tried to kill you?" He took the top off the pan, then dipped a spoon into the eggs, brought some out and tested the consistency, trying to look as if his heart weren't pounding. He felt protective, which brought with it a feeling of anger and helplessness. He wanted to keep her safe, but he didn't know if he could.

The eggs were done. Knowing he had to keep Alessandra here at all costs, he said, "Maybe we'll find some clues in my father's papers. We can start right after breakfast."

"You think we'll find something?"

"That's what I'm hoping," he answered as he served them each half the omelette.

One part of him desperately wanted that to be true. But the other part was much less sure, because finding a tie-in to the old murder would call Dad's detective work into question.

"How long was your father with the police department?'' she asked after they'd eaten in silence for several moments.

''Thirty years. He was the best they had,'' he said with conviction.

He heard her set down her fork. ''Then why do you think we'll find anything in his papers that will change things for Carlo?''

''Because of what I said last night. Somebody doesn't want us to look at the evidence,'' he clipped out, hoping she'd take the hint and drop the subject.

To his relief, she didn't try to make any more conversation as they sat at the table.

AFTER BREAKFAST, Alessandra helped Wyatt clean up the kitchen, pleased with how well they worked together.

She knew he was tense as she watched him rinse off the plates and set them in the dishwasher, and she wanted to go to him and slide her arms around him.

But his clipped conversation had made her feel uncertain about their relationship—uncertain about even her presence in his house.

After breakfast she called the carnival office from the phone in the kitchen. Milo was out, and Florica was the one who answered, so it wasn't a very satisfactory conversation. Finally, one of the other members of her extended family came on the line. It was Lila, who had stopped by the office to report that dogs from town had been into the carnival garbage. Alessandra asked her to see if Sabina could take over the fortune-telling tent for the evening. Then she left Wyatt's number and asked to have her sister call back.

When she made her way down the hall to the office, she saw Wyatt had pulled several file boxes from the closet. He was sitting beside them on an old but very lovely Oriental carpet, his arms drawn around his knees, his face pensive. When he heard her footsteps, he looked up quickly and blanked his expression, but she could tell that he wasn't looking forward to second-guessing his father.

"Here's the stuff," he said.

"How do we work this?" she asked, keeping her own voice matter-of-fact.

"Well, obviously I can't tell one piece of paper from another," he said. "I just know where Dad keeps his old work stuff. Usually, when I have an assistant working with me, I have him or her start looking through the folders—telling me what's there. If a document sounds relevant, then I'll scan it. Doesn't take long, because I have special equipment that can go through text quickly."

She hadn't touched him since he'd reached for her in the bedroom. Now she sat down beside him and laid her hand over his. At the pressure of her warm fingers on his flesh, he jumped.

"We can try something else," she said.

"Like what?"

"Like what happened in the fortune-telling tent. And then in my trailer. You said you could see what I was seeing."

He nodded tightly.

"Do you want to try that again—see if we can manage it?"

"It scared you, didn't it?" he asked.

"I don't think you liked it much, either!"

He gave a sharp laugh. "Yeah, it's difficult to handle. That's why I've kept my eyes closed around you."

"Like when we were making love?" she murmured.

"Yeah, like then."

The thickness in his voice made her turn her head, made her brush her lips against his. Just a light touch, to find out what would happen.

His arms came around her, pulling her to him, as his mouth took full possession of hers. At breakfast he'd acted distant, and she'd been afraid he was having second thoughts about the two of them.

The kiss told her what she wanted to know. He was far from indifferent. But circumstances were getting in the way—circumstances that tore at both of them.

She ached to pull him down to the surface of the carpet and show him what she was feeling. But the work they had to do was more important.

"Let's see if we can look at the folders together," she said.

She pulled one of the boxes toward her, removed the top and began looking at the names neatly written on the folder tabs.

She knew from the way Wyatt's breath caught and his muscles stiffened that he was using her vision now. Keeping her hand steady, she worked her way through the box, but there was no file that looked relevant.

In the next box, however, was a large envelope labeled Granville Murder.

With shaking hands, Alessandra pulled it out and started reading the material. It was a summary of the case, containing the facts she'd known for years.

"Are you reading with me?" she asked, hardly daring to believe it was possible that she and Wyatt were calmly sitting next to each other sharing this experience.

"Yes," he answered in a strangled voice, and she knew he couldn't quite believe it, either.

Familiar details leaped out at her. The body had been found at the edge of the swamp—near a large oak tree.

The murder weapon—a knife—was missing. Carlo Mustov had been having an affair with the victim—and the two of them had a fight the day of the murder.

Alessandra sighed. Nothing new.

As she turned the page, the phone rang. Wyatt broke the contact with her to answer it.

"Yes, just a moment," he said, holding the receiver toward her.

Scrambling up, she took the call. "Yes?"

It was Sabina. "Are you all right?" she asked.

Alessandra glanced at Wyatt. "It's my sister, calling me back."

"Go on and talk to her. I'll use the scanner."

"Thanks." Stepping into the hall, she said, "I'm fine."

"You don't sound fine."

"We found Wyatt's father's file on the Granville Murder. We were going through the material when you called."

"And?" Sabina asked tensely.

"So far, I don't see anything new."

"Well, what did we expect from Louis Boudreaux's son?" her sister snapped. "He's giving you the runaround!"

Alessandra lowered her voice and moved farther down the hall. "Sabina, he's blind, remember? I don't think he went into the office and removed stuff from the file. He couldn't see any of the materials. He didn't know what we'd find."

Her sister drew in a breath. "I'm sorry," she said. "I'm upset, that's all. Tell me he's treating you all right."

"He's always treated me just fine," she murmured.

"You slept with him last night!" Sabina said.

Alessandra felt her cheeks heat and was glad her sister couldn't see her face. "That's none of your business."

"It is, because I don't want to see my sister hurt."

"He won't hurt me," Alessandra answered, putting as much conviction into the statement as she could, even as she felt her chest tighten. She knew now that Wyatt wouldn't cause her pain on purpose. But she didn't want to talk about that, so she quickly changed the subject, asking Sabina to take over her job for a few days.

After her sister agreed, Alessandra asked anxiously, "What about my trailer?"

There was a moment's hesitation before Sabina said. "Well, it's totaled."

Alessandra had expected nothing less. Still, hearing it made her throat clog with tears.

Perhaps she made a small, choking noise, because her sister said, "Milo says that the carnival's insurance will pay for getting you a new one. And 'totaled' doesn't mean that everything's destroyed—just that the vehicle isn't usable. A lot of your things are okay. I've already taken some of your clothes to be cleaned."

"Thank you!" Alessandra replied, gratitude welling inside her.

They talked for a few more minutes. When she came back to the office, she saw Wyatt was using a scanner to read the pages. He'd set one aside, and as she walked toward him, she saw the troubled look on his face.

She'd been going to tell him about the trailer. Now she asked, "What's wrong?"

"Maybe nothing," he said, his voice strained. "I found some strange notations here that I'd like you to look at."

Chapter Six

Wyatt heard Alessandra cross the room, heard her pick up the sheet of paper he'd been holding.

At the bottom was a short set of numbers and letters—52PM.

"Looks like it could be a time. Maybe five-o-two in the afternoon."

"Which would mean what?" he asked sharply.

"I don't know."

"I think it's some kind of code." He answered his own question. "And I'm going to find out what the hell it is."

His pulse pounding, he reached for the phone again. As his hand touched the receiver, the instrument rang.

Beside him Alessandra gasped.

"What?"

"Something bad," she whispered.

"Oh, yeah? Something you and your sister arranged?"

"No!"

He pressed the button, listened as a woman began to speak.

"Is this Wyatt Boudreaux?"

"Yes."

"This is Emma Worthington, the manager at the West Bayou Nursing Home."

"Yes?" he said again, knowing from her voice that he wasn't about to hear good news.

"We called a couple of minutes ago, but we could only get your answering machine."

"That's because someone was on the line. What's wrong? Just tell me, for God's sake!"

"I'm sorry. The aide went in to give Mr. Boudreaux his lunch and discovered that he had…passed away."

Feeling as if he'd been punched in the stomach, Wyatt felt for the chair and sat down heavily. He felt Alessandra beside him, her fingers curling around his upper arm.

He closed his eyes, gripped the phone tightly.

"He went peacefully," Mrs. Worthington was saying.

Wyatt hoped to heaven it was true. "I'm coming over there," he said, then hung up and turned to Alessandra. "Can you drive me?"

"Yes."

He dug the key out of the desk drawer and handed it to her, then strode to the front hall and retrieved his cane.

Moments later he was beside her in the car as she backed into the street. He felt her hesitation, braced as she stepped on the brake too hard.

"Are you sure you can do this?"

"Yes! I just don't get much chance to drive, so I'm out of practice."

"Okay. Then turn right."

She did, then slowed to a crawl.

"What's wrong?"

"There's a police car parked at the curb. Should I tell him where we're going?"

"Yes."

She pulled up and rolled down her window, her conversation with the officer very brief. "Now where?" she asked Wyatt.

He thought about it. He'd never actually driven to the nursing home, since he'd been blinded before his father's stroke. But he knew the address and he remembered the location from when he'd been able to see.

Still, it was frustrating trying to give Alessandra directions. Several wrong turns made the trip take longer than it should have been.

He waited impatiently while she found a space in the parking lot, then almost tripped over a low concrete barrier at the edge of the blacktop.

Alessandra caught his arm, and he took a deep breath, using the cane more judiciously as he made his way to the front door.

"Mr. Boudreaux," Emma Worthington greeted him. "We're all so sorry."

"I'd like…to see my father," he said.

The woman hesitated, and he got ready to assert his rights when she said, "Yes. All right."

"Do you want me to come with you?" Alessandra asked.

"I *need* you to come with me," he answered, feeling his heart begin to pound as he started down the hall. He knew which room, the eighth one on the right. The door was closed.

"Yes."

He sucked in air and expelled it in a rush, wanting her to understand his overwhelming frustration, as well as his sadness. "I was going to ask you to come with me and meet him. I was going to question him. Ask him about the file. Ask him what he was hiding. Now it's too late for that. But…I haven't seen him since before the shooting that blinded me. If I can, I want to see his face—one last time. Will you help me do that?"

He felt her fingers clamp on his arm, heard the uncertainty in her voice. "I don't know why it's worked before. I don't know if it will work now. Maybe...maybe there are too many emotions in the way. I don't know...." Her voice trailed off.

"Or maybe it's our emotions that trigger it."

Before the incident in the fortune-teller's tent, he would have labeled his request as delusional. But they had taken this astonishing leap four times now. He didn't have the faintest idea why it had worked some of the times when they were touching and not others. He only knew that it was beyond any natural explanation. It was unexplainable—unless you conceded that he and Alessandra had forged some kind of supernatural bond.

"Just, please, can we try it?" he said, knowing that he was asking more of her than he had a right to ask. "Unless...unless it's too much for you."

"It's not too much. If I can help you, I will."

Still with his eyes closed, he felt for the knob, turned it and stepped into the room, aware every moment that Alessandra was right beside him.

"He's lying on his bed—like he's asleep," she whispered. "He does look peaceful."

"Yes."

She kept her fingers linked with Wyatt's as she took a step forward. He came with her, his pulse pounding in his ears so loudly that the sound seemed to fill the room.

He was afraid to breathe. Afraid to open his eyes. Afraid *not* to. When the tension became unbearable, he blinked them open.

To his profound relief, the miracle happened again. Only this time the wonder of it spread through him like the melody of a song he'd forgotten he knew.

He saw his father's face. The eyes closed, the features at rest.

"Can…can…you…?" Alessandra tried to ask, her voice cracking.

"Yes. God, yes." His fingers clamped on hers. When he felt her wince, he eased up the pressure. "Thank you," he managed.

The image blurred, and he knew that his eyes were filled with tears.

He closed his lids once more. "Thank you," he said. "I'll never forget this."

"I'm glad I could give you that gift," she whispered.

Probably she expected him to leave now. Instead, he walked toward the bed.

"Wyatt, we should go."

"He sent me to the carnival to get information. We didn't talk about what I found out. We've still got unfinished business."

"I understand," she said, but he was pretty sure she couldn't possibly understand.

"Maybe he left me something," he said, hoping it was true. He knelt, felt under the edge of the mattress. Then moved to the other side of the bed and did the same.

"Look under the bed," he said.

"All right," she said, sounding doubtful. But he heard her knees hit the floor. Moments later she reported, "There's nothing there."

"Try the nightstand. The dresser drawers. The closet."

"Okay." She still sounded doubtful, but at least she was willing to humor him.

He moved to the head of the bed, feeling under the pillow, and his fingers encountered a piece of paper. Pulling it out, he held it up. "I found something. You'd better tell me what it is."

Chapter Seven

Alessandra had thought they were on a wild-goose chase—until she saw the folded sheet of paper Wyatt held in his outstretched hand.

Quickly she crossed to him and took it. Unfolding it, she read, "Don't investigate the Gypsy murder."

He made a harsh sound that was somewhere between a laugh and a sob. "How convenient. Am I supposed to think he wrote that and stuck it under his pillow where I'd find it?" He sighed. "It's handwritten?"

"Block printing."

"So we can't go home and compare it to any of his notes."

"I guess not."

"I think we'd better assume that the same person who set your trailer on fire was here."

She sucked in a sharp breath. "Are you saying you think your father was murdered? To keep him from talking? And his death is supposed to be a warning to you?"

"His health was so poor, it wouldn't have taken much to push him over the edge. A pillow over his face would have done it. Maybe we'll never know. But I'm going to make sure they do an autopsy. And I'm going to question everyone in this damn place."

"Don't you think the police should do that?"

He stopped and ran unsteady fingers through his hair. "Yeah, I forgot. I'm not the police anymore, am I?"

She stepped toward him, took him in her arms. For a moment he held himself stiffly, then he cleaved to her, holding on tightly. When he finally spoke, his voice was gritty.

"Thank you for being here."

"For as long as you need me," she said, vowing to keep that promise.

She lifted her head. "Is there someone you can call? A relative who could help with the funeral arrangements?"

"My aunt Ida. She's in Los Angeles. And Aunt Stella. She's in Florida. It will take a while for them to get here."

"Then let me help you."

"Would you?"

"Of course. Tell me what I can do, and I'll do it."

IT HAD BEEN a dignified funeral. A moving funeral. An impressive funeral. Louis Boudreaux had been well-known in Les Baux. And well-liked. He'd been one of the town's leading citizens, and a considerable number of townspeople turned out at the San Michele Church to pay him tribute.

His son sat through the service and the interment in the family crypt wondering if his father's life had been a lie.

Since word had gotten out about his father's death, Wyatt had been inundated with well-meaning friends and relatives. He'd been waiting until the visitors were out of the way to take care of some unfinished business.

And finally it was time. The only person in the house with him now was Alessandra. They'd been sleeping in separate rooms, because he didn't want to damage her reputation any more than he already had. He knew from her phone conversations with her sister that her people couldn't understand why she was sticking with him. He wondered that himself, especially after the comments he'd heard from his aunts about ''that Gypsy woman he'd taken up with and what she might do while she was in the house.''

Alessandra must have heard them, too. And the remarks must have hurt, although she'd said nothing to him about them.

''Are you okay?'' she murmured as they faced each other across the living room.

''Yeah,'' he answered. ''I want to thank you. I know you've been keeping this place neat—so I wouldn't trip over anything people left in the middle of the floor.''

''Yes,'' she answered, but she stayed where she was.

He wanted to stride across the room and fold her into his arms—because he needed to, had needed to all week. But he didn't think he had the right to ask any more of her, so he stayed where he was.

''We haven't had much chance to talk,'' he said.

''I understand. You've been busy with other people.''

He cleared his throat. ''I appreciate your staying with me.''

''Do you?''

''What does that mean?'' he asked, more sharply than he intended.

''You haven't touched me. I was beginning to think you were just letting me stay around because you were worried about my safety.''

A low curse welled in his throat. Quickly he closed the distance between them and reached for her. And then she was in his arms, holding him, holding him tight. He kept his eyes closed, feeling the tension in her muscles.

"Oh, Wyatt, I thought you wouldn't let me close to you again."

"I wanted you to," he said, because he had vowed that he would only come to her with honesty. "But I didn't want to fuel the gossip."

"I've been…" She made a small anguished sound. "I thought maybe you were listening to the things people were saying."

"My God, you mean about you? The snide comments about Wyatt's Gypsy housekeeper? About whether she was going to steal the family silver?"

She nodded against his shoulder.

"You don't think I'd listen to crap like that, do you?"

"Well, it's not all that different from the…stuff I get from my family about you."

He laughed bitterly. "Yeah, probably they give you grief about 'the blind man.'"

"Yes. I want to wring their necks. But I try to be respectful, because I understand why they can't picture the two of us together. It's not because you're blind so much as that you're the son of Louis Boudreaux. The cop who helped convict Carlo."

"Yeah, wring their necks," he echoed. "That about sums up what I wanted to do with my well-meaning relatives. I would have, but I thought that getting into a brawl at my father's funeral would be…"

"Disrespectful?"

"Yeah."

He didn't know what else he could say. All he could do was cup the back of her head and angle her face so that he could bring his mouth to hers. It was a long, deep kiss, a kiss that helped bridge the gap that had grown between them in the past few days.

Then, sitting down on the sofa, she pulled him to the

cushions beside her. For long moments he sat there, just holding on to her hand.

Truthfully, he could have sat that way all night, just feeling close to her, maintaining the status quo. But they had important work to do.

Still, he wanted everything out in the open, so he said, "There are things we need to find out. Things about my father."

"Yes. I was wondering when you were going to tell me about the autopsy report," she finally said. "Did it come back from Baton Rouge?"

He blinked. That wasn't where he'd been going, but he took the question as a reprieve. Sitting up straighter, he told her what he'd learned.

"They ruled that it was 'death by natural causes.' Specifically, a cerebral hemorrhage. Apparently his blood pressure surged, and another blood vessel in his brain burst."

"You don't think that's how it happened?"

"I keep speculating, what if the same person who jumped me at the carnival had also paid Dad a visit the next day? There wouldn't have been any need for a physical attack. Dad was already weakened by one stroke. Some strategic intimidation would have done the trick."

"Do you have any evidence of that?" she asked, her tone telling him she didn't like where his thoughts were leading.

"No. Nobody at the nursing home heard anything. Nobody saw anyone who wasn't supposed to be there. But all that proves is that the staff wasn't paying attention to one sick old man while they got the ambulatory residents to the dining hall."

"So you're saying you think someone wanted to make sure he didn't talk?" she asked.

"I think so, yeah." He grimaced, speaking quickly now. "I've been waiting until people left. Now I need your help. Come into the office." Untangling his hand from hers, he strode down the hall.

She followed.

"Are the blinds closed?" he asked.

"Yes."

Probably she wondered what all this had to do with the previous conversation, and why he was going into the closet and pushing a filing cabinet out of the way.

"I've been studying up on the Theresa Granville case. And I've done a bunch of looking around the house—" He stopped and gave a harsh laugh. "At night, when my guests were asleep and I wouldn't disturb anybody. I found a door of some kind in here. I can feel the outline with my fingers, but I can't find any way to open it. Could you take a look at it for me?"

She came up behind him, and he felt her breast press against his arm as she leaned forward. For a moment he saw the wall. The image wavered, then abruptly cut off, and he knew this time she was the one who had closed her eyes. He felt a little shiver go through her.

"We could just stop prying into your father's private stuff and go up to bed and make love," she said in a shaky voice.

His breath caught. "Is that what you want to do?"

"Very much. Living with you all week and not being intimate has been…difficult. A couple of times I almost sneaked out of my room and into yours. But I didn't want to give your aunts any ammunition to use against the Gypsy woman."

He half turned and stroked his fingers down her arm. "When you're blind, you don't know who's watching you. If I'd been sure the coast was clear, I would have come to your room. But I didn't want to give them anything to talk about, either.''

"So here we are...alone," she said.

He ached to make love with her. Once more. Just once more—if that was all he could have with her. He almost pulled her into an embrace, but he stayed where he was. "The thing is, you might hate yourself in the morning."

"Why?"

"I remember when you didn't much like Louis Boudreaux's son, now we're going to find out how my father made sure your cousin got convicted."

She drew back. "You're certain of that?"

"The Gypsy murder was the most important case that ever hit Les Baux. If any case is tainted, it's that one."

"I guess we'd better find out," she whispered. "Do you happen to have a flashlight? I can't see much back here."

He laughed again, breaking some of the tension. "I didn't think about that. I'm pretty sure Dad had one in the utility drawer."

While she was off getting it, he sat with his hands balled into fists at his sides, wanting to get this business finished. Finally she returned, and he heard the light snap on.

"Well?"

She expelled a breath. "There's a seam in the wall. I guess you're right. It's some kind of rectangular covering—not exactly a door. There's no handle and no hinges." She was silent for several moments. "I think you open it by sticking something under the edge. A knife blade or a screwdriver."

"Do it!" he said, the order coming out low and angry. Damn his father! Damn him!

Again he could do nothing but wait for her to come

back, his tension and his frustration almost unbearable. He would have liked to do this in private, but that wasn't an option.

Again Alessandra returned, and he heard the scrape of metal against plaster, then a thunk as she set the covering down on the closet floor.

"Well?" he demanded.

"There's a recess inside. And some folders."

He didn't have to tell her to pull them out. "Let me get more light," she murmured as she stood and crossed to the desk.

He followed her, then began to pace the room. Maybe they could have tried the trick with the shared vision again. But he was too keyed up to sit still.

"What are the folders?" he asked.

"They, uh, they don't have names. They have letters and numbers—like the ones you found on the folder before the nursing home called."

"Is there one with the same notation—52PM?"

He heard her shuffling through the materials, then stop abruptly. "Yes," she whispered.

"What's inside?"

"Some of the same notes we saw before," she answered. "And...uh..." She gasped, sending a shock wave through him.

Chapter Eight

Alessandra stared at the photograph buried among the notes.

"What have you found?" Wyatt demanded, coming up behind her and cupping her shoulders with his hands—making contact. And she knew at once what he was doing.

They had done it before, shared her eyesight. And each time had been like stepping into another universe where the physical laws were beyond her understanding.

Bending her head, she stared down at the crisp, color image lying on the desk.

She was looking at a photograph of a piece of jewelry. An intricately made brooch with small red and white stones worked into a flower design. Rubies and diamonds. She knew that from the newspaper articles that had been written about the murder.

The leaves around the flowers were gold. And on one she could see a mark. It was clearly a fingerprint.

A bloody fingerprint.

Wyatt sucked in a sharp breath.

"You're seeing what I see?" she asked, although she didn't really need confirmation.

"Yeah. I believe so. You're looking at Theresa Granville's famous brooch, the one she was wearing the night she was killed. It was one of the chief pieces of evidence tying Carlo to her—because it was found in his bedroom.''

''Yes,'' she breathed. The facts of the murder had been burned into her consciousness.

''Of course, when it was found in Carlo's room, there was no mention of a bloody fingerprint,'' he went on, like an instructor at the police academy presenting a case to the students. ''So now we have something that didn't come up in the trial. Something Detective Louis Boudreaux knew about but excluded from the official report.''

''Why would he do that?''

Wyatt made a low, angry sound. ''Because he assumed Carlo was guilty—and he wanted a conviction. I'd be willing to bet this isn't Carlo's fingerprint. That would have been a little inconvenient at the trial—trying to explain why Theresa's jewelry bore somebody else's bloody fingerprint.''

''It could be *her* fingerprint,'' Alessandra said, still trying to come to grips with this new development.

''I'd be willing to bet it isn't.''

''You're saying your father deliberately withheld this photograph?'' she asked carefully.

''Yeah. That's what I'm saying. There's a term for it. It's called exculpatory evidence. Evidence that would tend to exonerate the accused. My father withheld the photograph so it wouldn't interfere with your cousin's conviction.''

The pain radiating from him was more than she could bear. Setting down the photograph, she turned and wrapped her arms around him.

He made a strangled exclamation. ''Don't you get it? My dad—the fine upstanding cop—withheld evidence that might have gotten your cousin off.''

"And you had the decency and…and the guts to find that evidence and share it with me. Even when you were afraid of what you'd find, you went ahead."

He gulped in air. "Everything I thought about my father was false."

"Don't say that. Probably he thought he was doing the right thing."

"You're defending him?" Wyatt asked, his tone incredulous.

"No. But I understand why he did what he did. Carlo was a troublemaker. He was having an affair with a married woman. The wife of the mayor. That would have been bad enough if he'd been a local guy. But he was one of the Gypsies."

"Don't make excuses for my father," Wyatt said harshly.

"I'm not. I'm just trying to tell you I understand." She pressed her head against his midsection, speaking rapidly, desperate to share what was in her heart. "And I want you to know that your letting me see this photograph overwhelms me. You are so strong, Wyatt. Another man would have left this evidence where it was. You were pretty sure you weren't going to like what you found. But that didn't stop you."

His voice was low, barely above a whisper when he answered, "I became a cop because I believe in upholding the law. That hasn't done me much good."

Lord, she knew what he meant. It had gotten him blinded. And now it had made him lose respect for his father—a man he had obviously idolized and loved deeply. In her eyes, that only made his own sacrifice all the more heartrending.

"Maybe we'll find out that this evidence doesn't mean what we think it means."

"I wouldn't bet on it." Wyatt sighed. "I've got friends in the department in New Orleans. I'll get them to run the fingerprint."

"Yes. Thank you."

"Don't thank me yet. It might not amount to anything."

"Wouldn't it make them reopen the case?" she asked in a shaky voice.

"I don't know. They might have some way to get around it."

She hesitated then, wanting to say more, but afraid to take the next step. Finally she decided that she didn't have much to lose.

"I'd like to tell Valonia," she said.

"It might give her false hope."

"I'll take that chance. And...and I have another reason." She plunged ahead. "It might make them see you differently. You didn't let prejudice against my people stand in the way of helping my cousin. And you didn't let your feelings for your father stand in the way, either. I want them to understand that."

He sighed again. "It might not make any difference."

She looked at her watch. It was after midnight, and the carnival would be closing for the evening. "I'd like to tell them," she persisted. "I'll go out there and do it now. Then I'll come right back."

"No!"

"You want to keep the evidence a secret?"

He shook his head. "That's not what I mean. I don't want you at the carnival by yourself. If you go, I'll come with you."

She thought about that. "All right. But would you be insulted if I asked you to wait outside when I go in to talk to Valonia?"

"No. I understand why. But we'd better put this back where we found it before we leave. I wouldn't want it to disappear."

"You think it could?"

"Yeah," he muttered.

They replaced the folder in its hiding place, and Wyatt pushed the filing cabinet back into place. Then they went outside and climbed into his father's car.

The ride to the carnival took about fifteen minutes. It wasn't far from town, she mused as they pulled into the parking lot. But it might as well be in another universe.

Suddenly she was felt uncertain. She'd been outraged by the way the authorities had treated Carlo. They'd seen him as Gypsy riffraff from the carnival, and in their minds that had made him guilty of murder. Her anger had grown as the trial had progressed and he'd been convicted. But her anger was nothing compared to his mother's anguish.

Valonia had never been the same since Carlo's death sentence. How would she react now?

There were still vehicles in the parking lot when they arrived at the carnival grounds. Unfortunately teenage boys with nothing better to do were tooling around, some of them driving pretty fast.

"What?" Wyatt asked as she pulled him out of the way of a battered sedan.

"Kids hot-rodding," she replied, wondering why the police didn't come out here and send the young men away—before two of them crashed into each other. Or they hit one of her people.

Wyatt kept hold of her arm as they stepped onto the darkened midway, the wood chips cushioning their steps as they passed the closed booths.

She slowed when they neared the fortune-teller's tent.

She hadn't been there in days. Valonia and Sabina had taken over for her, and she was grateful.

Now she hoped she could do something for her aunt.

They turned onto the lane that led to the family trailers. When they passed the spot where her own home had been, she gasped.

"What?" Wyatt asked again, and she heard the frustration in his voice.

"My trailer's gone. I knew it would be. But it's different seeing the empty space. It's like I don't belong here anymore," she murmured, then cut off the words abruptly, wondering if they made Wyatt uncomfortable.

Since arriving, she'd felt uncomfortable herself. Actually, stepping back into her own environment made her realize how little chance she and Wyatt had of staying together on any long-term basis.

She was from the carnival. He was from town. And the two had never blended. Such as when Carlo had had an affair with Theresa Granville.

She tried to shake off the negative thoughts, realizing that she wasn't in the best frame of mind for making critical evaluations.

Still, it was almost a relief when they arrived at Valonia's trailer and she could ask Wyatt to wait for her.

"Of course," he answered.

When she heard the edge in his voice, she wondered if he was having thoughts similar to hers. Well, they'd deal with their personal problems later. Right now, she was going to talk to her aunt.

Her knock on the door was answered with a low, "Come in."

She stepped into the hallway and walked quickly to the living area.

Valonia was seated on the small sofa under the back

window. The room reflected the flamboyant tastes of their people. The sofa was covered with a bright rectangle of red-and-yellow fabric. The rug had an intricate flower pattern.

But none of those dominated the room. Instead, what drew the eye was the wall of photographs, all of Carlo. They showed him as a baby, a child, as a teenager, a young man working at the Ferris wheel. In a cluster by themselves were the photos of him that had appeared in the paper after his arrest and conviction.

Some of the older photographs were enlarged and framed in gold. Others were snapshots gathered into carefully arranged groupings.

Valonia's hawklike eyes fixed on Alessandra. "I'm glad to see that you've returned to your senses. It's about time you left that man and came back to your people. He's worthless. Blind. He got what he deserved."

At the older woman's callous words, Alessandra's insides churned, but she kept her features calm out of respect for her aunt. "Don't say things like that. Wyatt isn't worthless. He helped me discover something that may help Carlo."

"I don't want to hear anything that man has to say. His father was our enemy, and he is, too."

Alessandra wanted to shout out a protest, but she understood her aunt's pain and managed to keep her voice even. "Don't judge him before you hear. He's been busy with his father's funeral, but as soon as he could, he went back to the materials from the murder investigation."

"Those papers are all lies!"

OUT IN THE HUMID NIGHT, Wyatt leaned toward the door, all his attention focused on the conversation inside the trailer.

When he hadn't been able to hear Valonia speaking, he'd opened the door a crack—then held his breath as he waited to find out if she suspected he was eavesdropping. But she was apparently too focused on her niece to pay attention to anything else.

He'd known that the old woman was angry. He hadn't realized the depths of her anguish. Apparently she wasn't able to listen to Alessandra's words, because the thoughts spinning around in her head were too powerful.

He wondered if it would help if he went inside.

Then he quickly discarded the idea. There was no way Carlo's mother could listen to him. If anyone was going to get through to her, it had to be someone she loved and trusted—Alessandra.

ALESSANDRA HAD almost reached the end of her rope. Firmly she said, "Valonia, please, listen to me. Don't jump to conclusions. Wyatt didn't just look at the official papers—he went searching for more evidence. And he found something his father had hidden. A photograph that shows Theresa Granville's brooch. The one they had at the trial. The one they said they found in Carlo's room. Only, this picture showed a bloody fingerprint on the brooch."

Her aunt stared at her as though she could hardly believe what she was hearing. "No! He wouldn't do that for you—for us."

Alessandra shook her head. "I know it's hard to believe. But he wasn't thinking about himself. He was thinking of Carlo—and of you."

Valonia looked stunned. "No," she said again. "No, it can't be true—I cursed the three of them. I cursed *him.*"

Alessandra felt her blood run cold. She knew of her aunt's rumored gifts. But she had never in her wildest imagination considered that Valonia had such power—or that she would have taken such a terrible step.

"You cursed him?" she breathed. "What curse?"

"I cursed them all. I said the words. I did the ceremony. Out in the swamp. I cursed the sons. Justice is blind," the old woman whispered. "Love is death. The law is impotent."

Alessandra struggled to catch her breath, trying to make sense of what she had just heard. "You're saying you were so angry that you did that to him? You made him blind?"

Her aunt's voice was steady. "Yes, I did it. I cursed him. And the others."

WYATT FELT HIS WHOLE BEING contract as he listened to the old woman.

She had cursed him? She had made him blind?

The woman in there—Alessandra's aunt—had taken away his life as he knew it?

Only a few days ago he wouldn't have believed it was possible. He'd been sure that one person's thoughts could have no physical effect on another, that there was no way the old woman could have done what she claimed.

He was a man who had always dealt in facts. In logic. In what he could verify with his own senses.

He'd had no belief in supernatural powers. But that was before his own recent experiences with Alessandra.

Sometimes when she'd touched him, against all reason, he'd seen what she was seeing. There was no logical way to explain what had happened. Yet he'd experienced it for himself.

What had happened between himself and Alessandra had been good.

What Valonia was talking about was evil. He felt a

choking sensation in his throat, in his lungs. At the moment he wasn't capable of rational thought. All he knew was that he couldn't breathe—and that he had to get away.

He had a good sense of direction. He had been here before. He turned and fled up the narrow lane, then bolted toward the right, up the midway toward the entrance.

In back of him, he thought he heard Alessandra calling. But he didn't stop. He had to get out of there. Away from the old woman.

He reached the parking lot and ran headlong across the open space—unable to see the car speeding toward him.

Chapter Nine

Wyatt heard the roar of an engine, heard tires spinning on gravel. Perhaps it was an illusion, but it suddenly seemed as if a vehicle was heading straight toward him.

He'd been running as fast as he could. Then he'd checked his forward motion, but it was already too late.

Metal collided with his body. His head cracked against glass.

The impact bought a scream to his lips. Then blessed unconsciousness took away the pain.

HE LAY ON CRISP SHEETS, his eyes closed. His head hurt. His body hurt, too, especially when he tried to take a breath.

"You're awake," an angel murmured.

No, not an angel. Alessandra. She'd been here with him. He vaguely remembered her presence hovering over him—loving and protective.

"How long since that car slammed into me?" he whispered, trying to squeeze the slender feminine hand that clasped his. He found he didn't have much strength.

"A day and a half," she answered, her fingers pressing his. "You've been conscious some of the time. We talked."

"My memory is kind of vague on that," he said, his voice rusty with disuse.

"Well, you had a concussion, a punctured lung and a broken leg."

"Dumb of me to run off like that," he muttered.

"You had a shock. We both did."

Speaking was an effort; so was staying awake. His eyelids fluttered, and he briefly saw the room, knowing it was from the contact of her flesh against his. Then he drifted off again.

Hours later, when he awoke once more, the pain was less.

"Hello again," Alessandra said. Her fingers were still wrapped around his.

"You should go back to my house and get some rest," he said.

"They brought me a nice comfortable chair. You know, special treatment for someone visiting a decorated ex-cop. I've had plenty of rest."

He opened his eyes, blinked against the light. He and Alessandra were holding hands, so he could see her.

She was sitting in a fake leather chair, wearing a deep blue dress that looked wonderful against her creamy skin.

"It's nice to wake up to such a beautiful sight," he said. "I love that dress on you."

She glanced down at her lap, but the view didn't change.

"Let me tell them you're awake again." She got up and detached her hand. Quickly she crossed the room and exited.

He lay with his eyes closed until he heard footsteps again. Alessandra had brought a nurse, he saw when he opened his eyes, who checked his vital signs and told him he was doing fine.

With a growing sense of astonishment, he watched the woman work, watched her leave, then turned his gaze to Alessandra.

"I saw that nurse," he said, his voice low and husky. "I can see you now. I thought when I woke up that it was because you were holding my hand. But that's not it. I'm seeing you—on my own," he said, still not quite believing it.

She ran to his side. "Oh, Wyatt! Are you sure?"

He laughed, ignoring the pain, his gaze focusing on the front of her dress. "Hmm, you need proof? Well, from this vantage point, it looks like you're wearing a bra under that beautiful blue dress. Too bad. I'll just have to take it off you when I'm a little stronger."

She reached for him. And he had enough strength to bring one arm around her. There was no need to hold her to him. She stayed right where she was, clasping him gently yet surely.

He felt her shoulders shaking, then felt drops of moisture hitting his face.

"Oh, Wyatt," she gasped. "I don't know how, but I think the curse is over for you."

"I think a nice smack upside the head may have had something to do with it," he whispered, taking care not to laugh this time.

"Maybe it's love," she whispered. "And maybe it's that you made a tremendous sacrifice for me. You could have hidden the evidence that your dad withheld. But you went looking for it—for me." Her arms tightened around him, but carefully, so that she didn't hurt him. "Oh, Wyatt. I love you so much. I always did. But I was afraid to admit it, even to myself."

Hearing those words made his heart soar. "I loved you, too," he answered, his throat thick. "I love you now. But

I thought it was hopeless. So I tried to tell myself it wasn't true.''

When her fingers tangled with his, he held on to her with all the strength he possessed, thinking that he and Alessandra had already wasted too much time. ''So, now that we've both admitted we were fools to call it quits last time, does that mean you'll marry me?'' Realizing what he'd said, he held his breath.

''Oh, yes,'' she answered immediately.

He sighed out his relief.

For long moments she clung to him. Then she pulled back and wiped the tears from her eyes.

''Now that you're my fiancée,'' he said thickly, ''I can rest easy.'' He was asleep again as soon as he finished the sentence.

The next time he awoke, he heard a woman's voice. When he opened his eyes, he saw that Alessandra was talking to the nurse. ''I'm back,'' he said.

Alessandra hurried to his side, smiling, then stepped aside so the nurse could check his vital signs.

Then he and the woman he loved were alone again.

''I didn't dream that, did I?'' he asked carefully. ''You said you'd marry me?''

''I did.''

He smiled. ''Then how about a kiss?''

She leaned down and touched her lips to his. Stronger than he'd been the last time, he held her to him, deepening the kiss, his soul warming at the contact.

At last she straightened, smoothed her hair.

''I'll muss you up a little better when I get out of this hospital bed,'' he said.

God, she was pretty when she blushed, he thought. Then he grew serious again. ''So, should I buy a trailer and move around with you? I figure I can work as a P.I. And I can do that anywhere.''

"You'd live in a trailer?"

"For you, I'd live in a pup tent."

She reached for his hand, held tight. "When you took me home, I loved your house. I loved the garden. And the big rooms. Living in a house like that would be like stepping into a dream world. Living there with you would be…wonderful."

"Hmm, it will be fun to see you decorate it."

"You don't mind my making changes?"

"No. I'd love your making the place your own."

She looked pleased, then her expression sobered.

"What? Whatever you're thinking, tell me!"

"Would you mind traveling with the carnival part of the time? At least at first. I'd feel like I was leaving them in the lurch if I disappeared. There's a girl who can take my place. My cousin, she has the talent to be a good fortune-teller, but I need to train her."

"I'd like living with you there—if your family can accept Louis Boudreaux's son."

"They know what you've done for us."

"They know my father hid evidence that would have cleared Carlo," he said, knowing he had to get that out in the open, yet feeling his insides clench as he waited to hear her response.

"Wyatt, what you did—showing me that evidence— took courage and integrity. Your father gave you those qualities because of the way he raised you."

"But his life was a lie!"

"Or he just made one big mistake. Don't judge him. You don't know what kind of pressure was put on him."

"You can say that?"

"Yes. I can. Remember, I was the woman who hated

you for the wrong reasons. It was such a relief when I gave up that hate. Like lifting a terrible weight off my shoulders. Nobody knows better than I do that we have to go ahead from here. Loving each other. Supporting each other. Focusing on everything good in our lives.''

He nodded, understanding that it was true, understanding how lucky he was. He had his sight back, and he was going to marry the woman he loved—a woman who could make his life complete.

"Don't let bitterness eat at you. Promise me."

He swallowed. "I can't do it all at once. But with your help, I can start."

"Do it for yourself—not me. I give you permission to forgive him."

He nodded, amazed at how wise she was and praying he could accept the challenge she'd thrown to him.

"Let's start with love," he said. "How about another kiss?"

"As many as you want!" She leaned over, pressing her lips to his, then deepening the contact, and he knew he was the luckiest man in the world.

SABINA

ANN VOSS PETERSON

To Denise O'Sullivan, Rebecca York and
Patricia Rosemoor for asking me
to be part of *Gypsy Magic*.

And to Rebecca, Patricia and Norman
for all the fun we had exploring the bayou.

Chapter One

Sabina King stepped back from the opened hospital door before her sister and Wyatt spotted her. She had heard their words of love, spoken only for each other's ears. She had seen the joy in their faces, happiness after years of pain and suffering and longing. And she wasn't going to get in their way.

Not this time.

No matter what Alessandra had said about her reasons for sending Wyatt away all those years ago, Sabina knew she'd been at least part of the reason her sister had given up the man she loved. And now that Alessandra and Wyatt had found each other again, Sabina wouldn't interrupt even a moment of their time together. They deserved time alone. Time to explore their feelings. Time to plan their future together. Time to heal.

Blinking back tears of joy for her sister, Sabina forced herself to turn away and walk down the long, white corridor. The heels of her sandals clacked on the tile floor. The green and indigo gauze of her skirt danced and swirled around her legs as she walked. Nurses, orderlies and visitors alike turned to watch her pass. Their eyes narrowed with suspicion or curiosity or a mixture of both. She could read the emotions in their faces and in the band of glowing light surrounding each person. The aura, which was her gift to see and interpret. She knew what they were thinking. The Gypsy. The fortune-teller. The thief.

Of course, they were wrong about everything but the Gypsy part. She was no fortune-teller. Not really. That gift had eluded her. That gift had been bestowed on Alessandra alone.

And Sabina was no thief. Though some probably thought the simple healing spells and charms she sold at the carnival were a kind of thievery. Spells and charms Valonia had taught her after Sabina had returned to the carnival six years ago in shame. Taught her so she could make a living. And have a purpose.

Sabina drew a deep breath, trying to purge the negativity from her thoughts. She knew what Alessandra would say. She'd say Sabina had a purpose. A purpose more powerful than seeing the future. More powerful than reading auras. More powerful than the simple spells she sold. A gift as powerful as life itself.

She looked down at her hands, swinging by her sides as she walked. Hands that could absorb another's injury. Hands that could heal. Heat crept up her neck and spiraled through her mind. She raised her eyes and focused straight ahead, striding faster until she was nearly running down the corridor.

What good was her gift if it couldn't be controlled? If it couldn't be used? What good was her gift if she couldn't heal Wyatt's injuries? If she didn't dare try?

Her fear wasn't the only thing holding her back. There were other forces at work in Wyatt's case. Forces she didn't understand. Wyatt had told Alessandra he could see again. Valonia's curse—the curse Alessandra had told her about—was broken. And Sabina couldn't risk that her attempt to heal him of the injuries sustained in the accident would not only bring back his health, but the curse, as well.

But with Wyatt lying in a hospital bed and Alessandra by his side, who would prove Carlo was innocent? Who would deliver him from that horrible Louisiana state prison in Angola, where he waited on death row? Who would save him from being strapped to a gurney in less than three weeks and having a fatal needle plunged into his arm?

Sabina pushed open the wide glass door and walked out into the damp heat. She might not be able to heal Wyatt, but there was something she could do. She could continue what Alessandra and Wyatt had started.

She could save Carlo.

THE WINDOWS of the once-grand house on the outskirts of Les Baux seemed to stare into the twilight, dark as soulless eyes. Sabina shivered despite the thick blanket of heat and humidity lingering from the day, and forced her feet to move step by step up the winding walk. The stones tipped, uneven under her sandals. Birds flitting around the house and in the garden sang the end of the day, their music almost mournful in the stillness. Wisteria vines covered the house's stone walls, their pendulous flowers long since wilted and dried by Louisiana's summer sun. The hard knot of apprehension tightened in her stomach.

She'd spent the entire day at the courthouse, trying to convince someone, anyone to listen to her about the photograph of the bloody fingerprint Alessandra had given her after Wyatt's accident. The one Wyatt and Alessandra had found in Wyatt's father's files. But the only answer Sabina had heard was no. The only advice was to "go through proper channels." The only response was the old familiar suspicion and mistrust.

She shook her head and kept walking. How could she go through proper channels? Carlo's public defender was long since dead. And although a law student here and a pro bono attorney there had helped him file appeals throughout the ten years he'd languished on death row, they had ceased returning Valonia's phone calls long ago. And her calls to other attorneys had yielded the same response. They couldn't handle another pro bono case. There was nothing they could do. Carlo had exhausted his appeals.

Her cousin had run out of time.

And that was what had brought her to this house. A search through the register-of-deeds office had provided the address of the district attorney who'd prosecuted Carlo ten years ago. She only hoped he would listen. Only hoped he wouldn't brush her off with talk of "proper channels" and narrowed eyes of suspicion. Because if he didn't listen, she didn't know where to turn.

She stepped onto the wide porch, the wood thumping under her feet as loudly as her pulse thumped in her ears. Crossing the porch, she strode to the front door and seized the large brass knocker.

The clack of brass against wood echoed through the house. She held her breath and strained to hear movement from inside.

The sound of feet striking wood flooring reached her. The doorknob turned, and the door opened. Face shrouded in shadows, a man looked out at her. At first she could see only his eyes. Dark as sin and rich as chocolate, they penetrated the shadows and seemed to look straight into her soul. Then the twilight's glow fell on an angular face tapering to a strong jaw.

Sabina's heart jolted. She'd seen him before—she was sure of it—long ago, when he was just a gangly boy walking the carnival midway in search of fun on a summer evening. Their eyes had met across the crowd. And later, when a gang of town boys had been harassing her, he'd come to her aid, ordering them to leave her alone and backing up the order with an intense stare that sent the boys off to find an easier target.

Although the contact had lasted but a few minutes, the protectiveness in his eyes and the brilliance of his aura told her everything. In a glance she'd known him better than she knew her own heart.

"You're from the carnival, aren't you?"

His voice didn't carry the sneer of most townsfolks' voices when they identified her as part of the carnival. But after hearing that sneer so many times and seeing the narrowing of their eyes and the way they clutched purses and fingered wallets, she couldn't help raising her chin just a little in defiance and straightening her spine as if readying herself to fight. "Yes, I am from the carnival."

He looked at her now with eyes so intense, they seemed to drill into her. "I remember. You sold charms for your aunt. Healing spells." The corners of his lips crooked up with the hint of a wistful smile. But there wasn't anything wistful in the aura she read. No longer the brilliant glow, it was weak, uneven, the color subdued. He was wounded somehow. Crippled.

What had happened to the boy who'd defended her all those years ago? The boy she'd thought about many times in the years since?

"Can I help you?" His voice startled her out of her thoughts.

"I've come to speak to Claude Rousseau." Her voice sounded weak and shaky, its volume barely rising above the pounding of her pulse. "This is Claude Rousseau's home, isn't it?"

"It sure is." The man pulled the door open wider and held out his hand. "The name is Garner."

"Sabina King." She placed her hand in his. His grip was steady, his hand neither smooth nor overly rough with calluses. And as his skin pressed against hers, a warm feeling spread up her arm and curled inside her, low in her belly. So like the feeling she'd gotten years ago when she was still a girl, when her gaze had first met his across a crowded midway.

He held her hand too long for a simple handshake, as if he was as reluctant as she to break the contact. And when he finally did release her, the lines around his eyes and mouth seemed to deepen with regret. "So why do you want to see my father?"

His words jarred her like a splash of icy water. "You are Claude Rousseau's son?"

"Unfortunately, yes."

The words of Valonia's angry curse echoed through her mind. *Justice is blind. Love is death. The law is impotent.* So the boy she'd never been able to chase from her imagination was Claude Rousseau's son. The son of Valonia's curse. Was the curse responsible for his injured aura, the lines of worry and pain in his face?

She bit the inside of her bottom lip and kept the question to herself. It wouldn't do her any good to share it, that was certain. Even if Garner Rousseau believed her story about Valonia's curse, telling him he was cursed by the mother of the man she was trying to save was a sure way to blow any chance she had to save Carlo. "I need to talk to Claude Rousseau. I'll explain why I've come only to him."

"Only to him, *chère?*" Garner's lips pressed into a

bitter line. "Then I'm afraid you've come to the wrong place."

"Where can I find him?"

"The family mausoleum. My father died of cancer two weeks ago."

Chapter Two

Color drained from Sabina King's beautiful face, leaving a gray cast to her skin. The shoulders she'd thrown back in defiance when he'd asked if she was from the carnival slumped in defeat. "I'm so sorry," she said.

Garner reached out and grasped one of her arms, ready to catch her in case she pitched forward onto the porch floor. Her arm felt delicate under his touch, fragile. For a moment he was afraid it would break, the way her spirit had seemed to break at the news of his father's death.

His father had always been good at breaking people's spirits when he'd been alive. But never in a million years would Garner have thought the news of the old bastard's death would affect someone this way. He would have been far less surprised had Sabina King jumped for joy. "Is there something *I* can help you with?"

She shook her head, her dangling earrings tinkling with the movement. "I don't know. I'm...I'm so sorry for your loss."

"Thank you." Although she still seemed a bit disoriented, she seemed stronger, able to stand on her own now. Almost reluctantly, he released her arm. "Is there anything I can help you with? I'm trying to put his affairs in order."

She paused for a moment, worrying her bottom lip with her teeth. Finally she drew a deep breath. "I came to ask your father about a case he prosecuted ten years ago. My cousin was convicted of a murder he didn't commit. He's on death row. I was hoping your father could help."

"Help?" Garner nearly choked. "Unless you want to make absolutely certain your cousin gets the needle, my father wasn't the one to come to for help."

Those delicious lips pursed. Obviously not what she wanted to hear. "I don't know what to do. Your father was my last hope."

"Your last hope for what?"

"To get the courts to listen to me. I have new evidence. And they say I have to go through proper channels, and Carlo has exhausted his appeals, and I can't afford an attorney, and I don't know what to do. If I go through proper channels, I'm afraid it'll be too late. And then..." She stopped her rush of words, her breasts rising and falling under her loose dress. Her gold necklace jingled against the scooped neckline with each agitated breath.

Something had her upset, all right. Something his father had been part of. No surprise there. Claude Rousseau had a talent for upsetting people. Good, decent people, at any rate. And if Garner was any judge of character, he'd say Sabina King was a good, decent woman.

And a beautiful one, as well. Exotic. Colorful. So different from the monotonous gray his life had become. The monotonous gray he'd carefully cultivated to dull the pain.

He closed his eyes against her jade eyes and colorful clothing. He didn't need this reminder of how exquisitely beautiful life could be—and how exquisitely painful. He liked his safe, gray life. He needed it.

But he couldn't just stand by while his father made

innocent people suffer from beyond the grave. He'd caused enough suffering while alive. Garner opened his eyes and met Sabina's gaze again. If he could help her, he would. And when she left, he would retreat into his monotone world and stow his memories of her in a safe spot in the back of his mind. "Slow down and tell me what this is about."

"A murder that happened ten years ago." Her lips crooked into a cynical frown incongruous with the freshness of her face. "The Gypsy murder."

Recognition clicked in his mind. A person couldn't live within a hundred miles of Les Baux without hearing about the Gypsy carny who'd murdered the mayor's wife. The case had headlined newspapers and fueled the town gossip machine for months.

"My cousin Carlo is innocent."

"I'm sure he is." He was sure of no such thing, but it seemed a kind thing to say. If he remembered correctly, the carny had been in trouble before the death of the mayor's wife. Bar fights. Petty theft. The kind of activities that reinforced stereotypes that had followed Gypsies for centuries. But under the force of Sabina's sincerity, his doubts as to her cousin's character didn't mean much. He wanted to believe her. He wanted her to be right about her cousin. He wanted her cousin to live up to the faith she obviously put in him.

"I have evidence. Evidence the police covered up."

He shouldn't ask. He should wish her well with her evidence, bid her goodbye and close the door. He looked into her eyes. "What kind of evidence?"

She opened the folder she'd been clutching and held it out for him to see. After she'd explained the significance of the fingerprint in the photo and how she'd come to

ave the photo in her possession, she raised her gaze to
is face, searching his eyes for a response.

"Very interesting."

"You believe me?"

"Why wouldn't I? In Les Baux, police corruption is
bout as common as crawfish étouffée. But if I were you,
wouldn't stop there. The gumbo and jambalaya can be
ound in the D.A.'s office."

Her luscious lips quirked into a smile, despite her des-
eration. "Don't tell me. You're a chef."

"No. Just a public defender who likes to eat. And I
now what my father was capable of." Garner felt the
old familiar tightening in his gut at the thought of his
ather and what he did to clear cases and win himself
nother term in office. The evidence he manipulated. The
nnocent people he hurt. Innocent people Garner had spent
is career protecting. Innocent people like the woman be-
ore him. And maybe even her cousin. "And let's just say
our cousin would have been an ideal scapegoat."

A little crease formed between her eyebrows, as if she
vas mulling over his admission and formulating a plan.
'You said you're a public defender? That means you de-
end people who can't pay, right?"

His breath hitched in his throat. He knew where her
houghts were leading. And he couldn't go there. "I can't
ake your cousin's case. Although I passed the bar in Lou-
siana, too, I'm a public defender up in the St. Louis area.
Not here. I only came back to Les Baux to clean out my
ather's house and settle his affairs. I'll be here just a
ouple of weeks."

"But isn't this part of your father's affairs? He convinced a jury to convict my cousin for a murder he didn't
ommit. Convinced them to give him the death penalty."

His gut clenched. His father's lack of ethics and habit

of scapegoating people who couldn't defend themselves was the reason Garner had become a public defender. The reason he'd devoted his life to looking out for the little guy.

"You could work on his case just while you're here. Help me get a start. You wouldn't have to do any leg-work. Just tell me what to do and I'll do it. We'll work together. Please."

Just what he needed. To work side by side with this beautiful, exotic woman. Days going over court tran-scripts. Late nights drafting requests for appeal. His groin tightened.

Damn. He was in trouble. Deep trouble. And standing here—close enough to smell her fragrance, close enough to reach out and touch her—was only digging him in more deeply.

"Maybe I can help another way. My father's files are still in the attic. It's a mess up there. But we can take a look and see what he has on the case."

A small spark of hope ignited in her eyes, making them seem all the more electric, all the more dangerous. Dan-gerous because looking into her eyes made him want more. Made him feel alive.

"And I'll take you to see Leon tomorrow morning." The offer escaped his lips before he could bite it back.

She raised her eyebrows in question. "Who?"

"Leon Thibault. He was my father's chief deputy. Now he's the district attorney in this parish. If anyone knows what went on ten years ago, it's Leon. Maybe we can pry some answers out of him."

"Thank you."

He forced himself to look away from her eyes, and swinging the door wide, he ushered her inside with a wave of his hand. "Don't thank me yet. We haven't found anything. And we might not."

She stepped past him and into the foyer. "I'm thanking you for your kindness. I haven't found much kindness lately. It's a welcome gift."

"I can't imagine anyone being unkind to you." Just looking at her made him want to do anything to help her. No matter what the cost to himself.

A sad smile flitted over her lips. "Unfortunately I don't have to imagine. People are unkind to Gypsies as a matter of course, it seems."

He nodded. "Yes, I remember."

She crooked a slender brow in question.

"The night we first met. At the carnival. The Breton boys were being unkind, if I remember correctly."

Her lips curved in another smile. But this wasn't one of sadness. This one was intimate with shared memory. "You saved me from their pranks. That's what I remember. You stood up for me."

Garner's breath seemed to catch in his throat. He had. He'd been scared out of his wits, but he hadn't been able to walk away. Not when she was in trouble. "I couldn't believe they backed down and didn't just beat me to a pulp. I was so scared I must have been shaking for an hour afterward."

"You didn't seem scared. I remember thinking how incredibly brave you were."

He chuckled. "Oh, I was scared, all right. The only time I was more scared was once when I dove into the bayou on a dare. Thought I was going to drown before the alligators even had a chance to get hold of me."

Reaching out, she brushed his arm with her fingertips. "I guess I have even more reason to thank you, then."

The warmth of her touch lapped at his defenses. He

was crazy, looking into this case. Crazier than when he'd stood up to the Breton boys or dived into the bayou. Hell, being around her was more along the lines of diving into shark-infested ocean waters, no land in sight. But he couldn't help himself. He wanted to be around her, wanted to be around the color and life she exuded. Color and life he could never possess, but that he drank in, anyway, like a thirsty man drinks saltwater, knowing it will only make things worse.

Much worse.

EVEN WITH THE AIR conditioner blasting, the courthouse was warm and sticky as Sabina and Garner sat in the hallway outside the district attorney's office. She lifted her heavy hair off her neck with one hand. Damp tendrils framed her face and tickled her cheeks. At least she wasn't wearing a business suit like the deputy district attorneys rushing back to court after lunch recesses. How a person could wear something so confining in this bayou heat, she'd never understand.

She glanced at Garner sitting in the chair next to her. Dressed in a polo shirt and khakis, he seemed very cool, very relaxed. He'd helped her a lot already, staying up with her sorting through his father's files until the wee hours of the morning. Picking her up before noon at the carnival to drive her to lunch at the Bayou Vue Café in Houma and then to the district attorney's office. And waiting with her now.

She knew that Garner was dealing with issues of his own, issues that likely convinced him to help her with Carlo's case, issues to do with his father that she couldn't even begin to understand. But something inside her wanted to believe that there was more to his helping her than his need to right his father's wrongs. There was a bond between them. A bond far too strong to have been forged in the few hours they'd known each other. And she wanted to believe he felt that bond as strongly as she did.

She shook her head, trying to chase the ridiculous thoughts from her mind. She wasn't a silly romantic girl anymore. Not as she'd been when she'd first laid eyes on Garner. For better or worse, she was now a woman. A woman who'd tasted the bitter flavor of failure, of rejection. A woman who didn't want to taste it again.

And Garner Rousseau obviously lived with his own pain, his own agony. It was in his injured aura, raw as an open wound. Something had happened to Garner Rousseau, too. Something horrible. And she could only hope her aunt's curse wasn't the cause.

"It looks like some things never change," Garner said, bringing Sabina out of her reverie.

She followed his gaze down the hallway. A gray-haired man in an impeccably fitted suit strode quickly away from them, as if he was making an escape out the back door. "Who is that?"

Garner's lips drew into a line. "State Senator Richard Granville."

Surprise darted through Sabina. "The husband of the woman my cousin Carlo was convicted of murdering?"

"The same. He was always tight with my father. Apparently he still has business with Leon."

Sabina didn't have time to digest what implications Richard Granville's appearance might have on the district attorney's willingness to hear her case on Carlo's behalf before the receptionist's lilting voice interrupted her thoughts. "Mr. Rousseau? Mr. Thibault will see you now."

Garner unfolded his powerful body from the chair and held out a hand to Sabina. "Ready?"

She took his hand and stood, clutching a folder in one hand, the copy of the fingerprint photo tucked securely inside. This was it. Maybe her last chance of saving Carlo from the injection scheduled to take his life. She had to focus on that. Not on the way Garner's touch made her feel. Not on silly notions of a mysterious bond they shared. This meeting was the important thing, and she couldn't blow it.

She released his hand and smoothed her palm over the straight black skirt she'd dug from the back of her trailer's closet this morning. She'd bought the skirt when her former husband, Joe, had insisted they shun everything Gypsy: the clothing, their names, and even the Gypsy purity code of *marime*. Right before he'd decided *she* was also one of those Gypsy things to be shunned. Raising her chin, she pushed past humiliation from her mind and faced the long hall to the district attorney's office. "I'm ready."

Garner nodded. "Let's go."

The district attorney was leaning a hip on his wide mahogany desk and flipping through a file when they entered his office. A wide nose, round, deep-brown eyes and the ruddy complexion of a Cajun who enjoyed his food and drink, Leon Thibault was younger than Sabina had expected, though he was probably one of those men whose age was hard to discern. And although the aura surrounding him was muddy and indistinct, a seemingly genuine smile lifted the corners of his lips as his gaze landed on Garner. "Garner, my boy. How are you holding up?"

Garner crossed the room and took Leon's offered hand. "I'm doing well, Leon. You know my father and I were never close."

Leon shook his head. "I know. I don't think Claude

was very close to anyone, truth be told. I just worried that his death would be hard on you on top of everything else that has happened.''

Pain registered in Garner's aura. Drawing a deep breath, he waved Leon's words aside hastily, as if eager to rid the room of the utterance. "That's all in the past, Leon. All behind me. What we've come to talk to you about today is very much part of the present."

Thibault nodded and for the first time since they'd entered the room, his gaze landed on Sabina. "Though it started in the past, from the sound of your message this morning. You want to talk about the Gypsy murder, is that right?"

A damp shiver crept over Sabina's skin, following the path of Leon Thibault's gaze. She nodded. "I have new evidence. Evidence that shows that someone besides Carlo Mustov murdered Theresa Granville."

Thibault's bushy brows crooked toward his receding hairline. "Evidence? Of another murderer? Excuse my doubt, Miz King, isn't it? But I worked on that case, and that Gypsy boy was guilty as sin." He slurred the words as if to imply all Gypsies were guilty merely for being Gypsy.

She drew in a deep breath. She hated referring to non-Gypsies by the term *gadje*. Even though the term wasn't inherently disrespectful, it seemed bitter. A reaction to the oppression and prejudice the Romany people—or Gypsies—faced over the centuries. But in some cases—bigots like Leon Thibault—she felt the term was justified. She raised her chin and looked him straight in the eye. "My cousin Carlo is innocent. And I have proof. Evidence the police withheld."

"Let me see this evidence."

Swallowing hard, Sabina handed him the manila folder.

He flipped the cover open and reached for a pair of reading glasses on his desk. He perched the spectacles on his nose and studied the photo and report in front of him. Raising his gaze, he peered at her over the lenses and shook his head.

Sabina craned her neck over the edge of the folder and pointed to the photo. "It's a bloody fingerprint on the brooch. Theresa Granville's ruby-and-diamond brooch. The one she was wearing right before she died."

"I can see that. The brooch that was found in your cousin's trailer."

"Yes. But the fingerprint doesn't belong to Carlo or Theresa. Someone else touched that brooch. Someone else had Theresa Granville's blood on his hands. Someone else killed her."

Thibault shook his head. "You're getting ahead of yourself, Miz King. This fingerprint means nothing."

His words hit her like a kick to the head. "Nothing? This fingerprint means Carlo is innocent. He's going to die for something he didn't do."

"Nonsense."

Garner stepped to Sabina's side. "What are you saying, Leon? This seems like pretty good exculpatory evidence to me."

Thibault tore his hard glare from her and focused on Garner. His mouth turned up in the corners and his eyes softened as if he was addressing a favorite nephew. "Yes, under normal circumstances, it would be. But this is far from normal."

"Far from normal?" Sabina parroted. "What do you mean?"

The impatient glare returned to his eyes, along with a cocky grin. "I mean that evidence like this might be enough to convince the appellate court to grant a new trial...if it was real.''

If it was real? Anxiety gnawed in the pit of Sabina's stomach. ''The police had this photo ten years ago, but buried it. It was sent to the lab for identification last week.''

''Really?''

''Yes.''

''And the fingerprint was identified?''

''No. They couldn't find a match. But they determined it wasn't Carlo's print.''

''Of course it wasn't. And did the lab determine the blood type of this bloody fingerprint?''

''No. They didn't have a chance to. Someone had wiped the brooch clean. This photo is all that's left.'' Why was he asking all these questions? The photo said it all. ''The police wanted to convict my cousin. When they couldn't identify the print on the brooch as Carlo's, they wiped it off the jewelry and hid all evidence that it existed.''

''A logical assumption if you don't know the entire story. Let me fill you in on something, Miz King. The print wasn't identified because it wasn't supposed to be identified. And ten years ago the police didn't have the lab test the blood for type because it wasn't Theresa Granville's blood.''

She shook her head in confusion. She wasn't following him at all. ''Wasn't *supposed* to be identified? Wasn't Theresa's blood? What are you talking about?''

''I was at Carlo Mustov's trailer that night, Miz King. I saw the jewelry when the police found it. And, trust me, there was no bloody fingerprint on that brooch.''

Sabina's heart froze. ''No. That can't be true. If it is,

how do you explain this?'' She held up the photo of the fingerprint.

''The fingerprint wasn't hidden by the police to send your cousin to prison for a crime he didn't commit, Miz King. The fingerprint was planted on the brooch in order to get him acquitted.''

Sabina opened her mouth but couldn't force a sound from her throat. She just stared at Thibault, his words scrolling over and over in her mind. The aura around him was still muddy. He was lying. He had to be lying.

Garner skewered Thibault with a skeptical look. ''Why would someone want to do that, Leon? Mustov didn't exactly have a lot of friends in the police department.''

''No. The man was a troublemaker. But there was a detective on the case who was sympathetic to the Gypsies. I believe he was trying to protect Carlo Mustov.''

''Who? Give me his name.''

Thibault nodded. ''Certainly. Maybe you should talk to him. See for yourself.'' He glanced back down at the file on his desk, paging through it until he found what he wanted. ''The detective's name is Louis Boudreaux.''

Sabina's heart hitched and then fell somewhere in the vicinity of her toes. Louis Boudreaux, Wyatt's father.

Thibault turned back to her. ''Let me guess—he's the one who gave you this picture.''

Sabina didn't answer. She'd be damned if she'd let Thibault wrap his lies into a neat little bundle and tie a ribbon around them. ''I don't believe you. I think you're covering something up.''

He shrugged, palms out in front of him, signaling he had nothing to hide. ''Talk to Louis Boudreaux if you don't believe me. Ask him.''

''He died about a week ago.''

Leon Thibault's brows arched toward his hairline as if

he hadn't heard the news, but judging from the steady murkiness of his aura, he wasn't surprised in the least. He handed the photo back to Sabina. "I'm sorry I can't tell you what you obviously want to hear, but there was no bloody fingerprint on the jewelry or anything else we found in your cousin's trailer. If you don't believe me, I can get you a copy of the crime-scene report." Casting an apologetic glance in Garner's direction, he walked to his office door and opened it, signaling the end of their discussion. "Carlo Mustov is guilty of Theresa Granville's murder. And as a result, he will die."

"HE'S LYING."

Glancing at Sabina in the passenger seat, Garner started his car and pulled out of the courthouse parking lot.

He heard the tinkling of her earrings as she shook her head and repeated, "I know he's lying."

Garner focused on the asphalt road ahead, flanked by wide ditches of water, cattails and wild cane. "You saw the crime-scene report. Leon was at Carlo's trailer when the police searched it, just like he said. And like he said, there was no fingerprint found."

"Maybe he was there. But he's lying about the fingerprint."

"How do you know?"

She shifted in her seat and turned her head, looking out the side window at the mixture of humble trailers, grand brick houses and stretches of forest and swamp rushing by on the outskirts of town. "I just know."

"Women's intuition?"

"It's kind of like that."

"What is?"

"I see things that tell me how someone is feeling."

"Things?"

"Light. Energy. It radiates from people and changes color and intensity depending on how they feel."

"Auras. You see auras."

"Yes."

Garner had heard of the bands of light that supposedly surrounded every living thing. He wasn't sure he believed in auras, but he'd seen stranger things in his life. He supposed it could be possible.

"It's real."

He snapped his gaze to hers. "What?"

"It's real." She shrugged, her cheeks coloring softly. "I could see your doubt."

He refocused on the road. "That obvious, huh?"

"It was in your aura. An aura is a person's energy, that's all. Most people can feel it. And you can train yourself to see it, as well." She shrugged again. "I have a talent for it."

"What other talents do you have?" He didn't mean for the question to sound seductive, but it did, hanging in the air between them like a cloud of rousing perfume and strains of soft music.

Sabina hesitated before answering, as if she, too, felt the tension in the air. Finally she raised a hand and smoothed a strand of hair back from her cheek. "My family has many talents," she said, although it wasn't her family he'd asked about. "My sister can read the future. My cousin Andrei is empathic and telekinetic. And my aunt Valonia can cast spells." Her eyes latched on to his face. "And curses."

Thankfully, it didn't seem that reading minds was one of her talents. If it had been, she would know he didn't give a flying fig about her family's talents. He wanted to know about *hers*. Like how her body moved when she danced and what kind of feelings those lips could arouse moving across bare skin.

He mentally shook himself. There was only one place these thoughts could lead, and it wasn't a place he could go. No matter that the air between them sizzled with electricity.

He scoured his mind for a way to steer their conversation back to its original path, and away from the course his body wanted to lead it. "So you saw in Leon Thibault's aura that he was lying?"

"Yes."

"What part of his story was he lying about?" Garner struggled to keep his mind on Leon, but found himself watching her out of the corner of his eye. The strong lift of her chin. The way the sun glinted off her hair and highlighted the curves of her breasts under the gauzy top.

"I don't know. I couldn't tell that much from his aura. Only that something he told us was a lie. I can only interpret a person's energy. I can't read minds."

Garner expelled a relieved breath. Thank God for small favors. He forcefully pulled his mind from the landscape of her body and paid full attention to the flat ribbons of road and water ahead and the shadow of a truck in the rearview mirror behind. "Well, lying or not, unless we can find some evidence disputing Leon's story, we aren't going to get very far."

"We? Does that mean you'll work with me on Carlo's case?"

If only it could be that easy. If only he could help her, work side by side with her to save her cousin. But he knew damn well he couldn't. Her presence was like a drug to him, each dose increasing his addiction. And if he was foolhardy enough to help her, to spend more time with her, to get to know her, God knows what state he'd be in.

Even now the need to run his fingers along her cheek, to taste her lips, to draw some of her color, her life into his soul was eating him up inside. "I can't, Sabina. I'm sorry."

She pursed her lips and nodded slowly, as if she'd been bracing herself for his answer, as if she'd expected it. Shadows settled, dark as bruises in those beautiful green eyes.

He tore his gaze away. He couldn't look at her, couldn't witness the sense of rejection creasing her forehead and tightening her lips. He'd done his best. Given what he could. And he couldn't give any more. Not without endangering his heart. And hers.

He glanced into the rearview mirror. The pickup truck had caught up to them and followed close behind. The hot sun beat off the truck's tinted windshield and glared in his eyes. Damn truck was following too close. Much too close.

The palms of his hands broke out in a sweat. His pulse picked up its pace. He tried inhaling slowly in an attempt to ward off the fears. The memories of crushing metal. Of pain. Of loss.

First the excruciating desire to feel Sabina's touch, to smell her scent, to get to know her much better. And now this. He couldn't escape the memories. They were closing in on him. The sweetness he missed, and the tragedy that had stolen it all away.

Garner pulled well to the side of his lane to let the truck pass. But instead of swinging out into the oncoming lane, the pickup drew closer, its bumper nearly riding on the tail of Garner's car.

"What the hell?" Garner stepped on the gas, putting a few inches between them.

The truck roared ahead. Its bumper connected with his.

Garner's head snapped back against the seat. The steering wheel jumped in his hands. He clutched the wheel and struggled to regain control. "Hold on, Sabina."

The truck loomed, filling the rearview mirror. It withdrew a few inches and then rammed them again.

The car jolted and swerved to the shoulder. Garner fought with the wheel. He stomped on the brake, but it was no use. Gravel skidded beneath the tires. The edge of the water-filled ditch rushed to meet them. Just like before. Just like—

Sabina's gasp rent the air.

The car hit the water nose first, burying itself in mud and sharp stalks of cane. Garner's head snapped forward and then back against the headrest. Then there was no sound but the lap of water seeping into the car. The smell of the swamp clogged Garner's throat, thick as blood.

Chapter Three

"Sabina, please. Can you hear me?"

Sabina squeezed her eyes closed. She didn't want to open them. The light filtering through her lids was too bright, and her head hurt too much.

"Sabina, please. This can't happen again. Please." The voice cut through her foggy mind. A voice so full of desperation, so full of fear. Garner's voice.

She forced her eyes to open and focus on his face.

Garner was leaning over her, cradling her head in his hands. He was worried. Upset.

Alarm grabbed at her stomach. "What's wrong, Garner? Are you okay?"

A sound of relief whooshed from his lips. "It's you I'm worried about."

"Me?" The pungent scent of swamp hung in the air. Water seeped into the front of the car and inched toward her feet. Stalks of cane and cattails speared the sky, and the gleam of water surrounded the car on every side. Fear flashed back. The truck that was following too close. The truck that rammed their car and pushed them off the road. Pushed them into the water-filled ditch.

"You were so still. I couldn't tell if you were breathing at first." He smoothed her hair back off her face, his finers trembling. "I thought I'd lost you. Like Mary Ann. thought you were dead."

"I'm fine, Garner. Really." She wasn't sure if she was ne or not, but she needed to say something, anything to assure him. "Nothing broken. Just a little headache."

"Can you move?"

She sat forward in the seat. Her head spun as if she'd ist spent the entire day on Andrei's Tilt-a-Whirl. Forcing erself to stay steady, she looked at the encroaching water. I'm fine. Let's get out of here."

Clutching the dashboard with one hand, Garner pressed e seat-belt release and popped her belt free. "The ditch deeper on your side, so you'll have to crawl across the at to my side. Do you think you can manage?"

Sabina forced a smile to her lips, despite the timpani undering in her head. "No problem."

He grasped her hand, helping her across the seat and ut the driver's door. The water rose nearly to her waist, aking her long skirt cling and tangle with her legs as ie tried to wade to shore. Mud sucked at her sandals ith each step.

Garner slipped his arm around her and pulled her close. he heat of his body seeped into her like warm rain after long drought. And with it came a sense of strength. Of fety. Safety she had no business feeling after just being n off the road. And especially while wading through a tch that served as home to alligators and snakes. "Did u get a look at the driver of that truck?"

"No. I didn't get the license, either." He helped her p the bank to the shoulder of the road. "By the time I ally paid attention to the truck, it was too close to our ir to see the plate."

A bad feeling swirled inside her. First the man who tacked Wyatt, then the fire in Alessandra's trailer, and now this. Was the truck driver part of the pattern? Did someone know *she* was now pursuing Carlo's case? And was that someone set on keeping the truth under wraps? As they stood on the side of the road, she began to fill Garner in on her worries.

The more she told him, the more his alarm grew. "Did you report the attack and the fire to the police?"

"Yes. They wrote reports and that's about all that happened."

He nodded as if he'd expected her answer. "I'll see if I can give Les Baux's finest a little jump start when I report this." He nodded back in the direction of the car now settled more deeply in the ditch. "My cell phone is sleeping with the gators. The carnival isn't far. I'll call from there. Do you think you can manage the walk?"

Sabina nodded, the movement sending pain shooting down her neck.

Concern pinched Garner's brow. "Are you sure?"

"I'm sure."

"Lean on me. I'll help you."

She did as he ordered, reveling in the feel of his body against hers, his arm protectively around her shoulders. Ironically, even though he was taking care of her, she felt stronger than she'd felt in years. And more sure of herself. It was as if the touch of Garner's hand, the warmth of his body, brought out strength hidden even from her.

She only wished she could bring out the same strength in him. Garner's face was pinched with worry. And though his hands no longer trembled, Sabina could still see the anguish in his aura. The words he spoke after the crash echoed through her mind. "Who's Mary Ann?"

His arm tightened around her shoulders.

"You said her name. You said you thought you'd lost me. Like Mary Ann."

He didn't reply, just kept walking, the soles of his shoes grinding on the gravel.

She persisted. "Is this what the D.A. referred to? What you've been through lately?" She searched his eyes, but he wouldn't return her gaze. "It might help to talk."

He walked on, his eyes weary, his face drawn. Finally he cleared his throat. "Mary Ann was my wife."

Sabina nodded. A throb deep in her chest answered the pain in his eyes. "Did she die in a car accident?"

His gaze dropped to the gravel shoulder. "Yes."

Sabina swallowed into a dry throat. He'd lost his wife. His wife whom he obviously loved. How could he bear it? "When did this happen?"

"Six years ago. I still dream about the accident sometimes. Still try to make it turn out differently. I was making a left turn into the funeral home and the semi driver behind us wasn't paying attention. He never saw my signal. He never saw our car until he hit us and sent us across the road and into the drainage ditch."

Sabina's mind caught. "The funeral home? You were turning into the funeral home?"

"My mother had just died. A heart attack. We were scheduled to meet with the funeral director. To make plans."

Sabina's heart clutched. Valonia's curse rang in her ears. *Justice is blind. Love is death. The law is impotent.* "First your mother, then your wife?"

"And now my father. That makes everyone. Except me, that is." His mouth pressed into a bitter line.

Love is death. Was that the part of the curse that had befallen Garner? Had his wife and his mother died as a result of Valonia's curse? And though he'd clearly had big problems with his father, she'd never seen hatred in Garner's aura when he talked about Claude Rousseau.

Garner must have loved him. At least in some way. And now he was dead, too.

"My mother didn't trust doctors. She always said she couldn't stand them poking around. We didn't even know she had a heart condition. I keep thinking that if I'd forced her to have a checkup, she might still be here."

"You can't blame yourself. You couldn't possibly have known."

"Maybe not. But that's what we do after a tragedy, don't we? We go back and relive everything we did wrong. Every bad decision or little bit of neglect that led up to the tragic moment." He turned his head to look at her. A smile curled his lips, a smile that held no humor, only sadness and pain. "I guess I've just had more opportunities to second-guess myself than a lot of people."

"But none of it was your fault."

"My mother's death, maybe not. And my father's death. But Mary Ann's…" He shook his head and pulled his tortured gaze away. "I was driving."

Sabina shook her head. He couldn't blame himself. The cause wasn't what he'd done or failed to do. The cause had been dictated long ago by his father's actions and Valonia's revenge.

Sabina drew in a deep breath. "None of it was your fault, Garner. I know why everyone in your family died. Everyone you loved."

He met her eyes. "Why? Because God has a sick sense of humor?" His voice was bitter, angry. And she couldn't blame him. She couldn't blame him a bit. "There was no reason. I stopped looking for one long ago. Now I just want to find peace."

"There was a reason. Remember when I told you my aunt can cast spells and render curses?"

"Yes."

"When my cousin Carlo, her son, was convicted and sentenced to death, she put a curse on those responsible—those with sons, just like Carlo was to her."

His eyebrows crooked toward his hairline. "A curse?"

She nodded. *"Justice is blind. Love is death. The law is impotent."* She stopped walking and turned to look directly into his eyes. "Don't you see? Love is death. That is your curse. Those you love will die."

Garner looked down at her, his disbelief obvious.

"It's true," she said. "Believe it or not, whatever you wish, it's true. None of it was your fault."

He shook his head. Tightening his arm around her, he resumed walking along the highway's gravel shoulder. Finally he let out a sigh. "I don't know that your aunt is the source, but I do believe I'm cursed."

"Because you lost your wife, your family?"

"No. Everyone loses people they love. If that's a curse, then it's a curse the entire human race shares."

"If not your loved ones' deaths, then how do you believe you're cursed?"

"When Mary Ann died, I felt my heart was cut from my chest. It was two years before I could go even an hour without thinking of her, without wishing I had been killed along with her. I can't go through that again. Even if it means living alone for the rest of my life, I can't deal with the pain that comes with loving someone and losing them." He paused and looked down at her, his dark gaze cutting through what few defenses she had left and penetrating her heart. "But I never thought of it as a curse before. Not until now. Not until I met you."

Sabina's throat constricted. Her eyes burned with tears begging for release.

Garner looked away from her and focused on the road ahead. "We made it."

Sabina followed the path of his gaze. The carnival loomed in front of them on the outskirts of Les Baux. The Ferris wheel glinted in the sun as it turned, filled with families enjoying the day, enjoying each other. Sabina's heart ached at the sight.

Garner's arm dropped from her shoulders, but he didn't move away from her. He stood stock-still, looking out over the carnival. "I'll report the accident to the police. And I'll call a defense attorney I know who's due for a little extra pro bono work. He's good, and he owes me one. I'll have him contact you. If there's a way to help your cousin, he'll find it."

She nodded, her throat too tight to speak.

"I wish I could do more. But I just can't."

Pain pulsed from Garner like blood from an artery. Pain Sabina was powerless to heal. Pain that pulsed in her, as well. She reached for his fingers, wanting to renew the contact between them, then stopped and let her hand fall to her side, useless as a rag. "I guess this is goodbye."

"It has to be. I wish you luck, Sabina King."

She beat back her tears and looked up at him, trying to meet his eyes. But he didn't look at her. He kept his gaze on the Ferris wheel, as if turning his eyes on her one last time was too difficult.

"Thank you for your help, Garner Rousseau. I hope life gives you the good things you deserve from now on. You're a good man."

He forced a poor imitation of a smile to his lips. "Can you see that in my aura?"

She reached her hand toward him and rested it on his chest. He was so solid under her fingers. Yet so broken. "No, I can feel it in the beat of your heart."

GARNER WOVE and dodged his way through the late Friday-night crowd on the midway. Two days had passed since he'd said goodbye to Sabina. Two excruciating days of sitting alone at his father's house, sorting through years of memories and thinking about the scent of Sabina's hair, the tinkling of her earrings and the spark of life burning deep in her jade eyes.

He'd done everything he'd promised to do when they'd parted. He'd reported the pickup truck to the police and done his best to convince them to devote some time and effort to the investigation. He'd called the attorney friend he'd told Sabina about and enlisted him to work on Carlo's case. And he'd forced himself to stay away from Sabina, though nothing he could do would chase her from his thoughts.

He'd been over and over his decision to let someone else help Sabina with Carlo's case. And each time he reviewed what he'd done, he knew he'd made the right choice. He'd only spent two days with Sabina. Two days. And already she'd burrowed under his skin and was working her way dangerously close to his heart. Any more time with her and he didn't know whether he could stand saying goodbye. And he couldn't let that happen. He couldn't face that kind of pain again. He had to watch out for himself this time. And for her.

But for the past few days, he hadn't been able to think of anything but the truck bearing down on them on the highway, the fire in Sabina's sister's trailer and the knife attack on Wyatt Boudreaux. He had to see her one more time. He had to make sure she wasn't taking risks to find more evidence to exonerate her cousin. Risks that could jeopardize her safety. Maybe even her life.

But as soon as he made sure she was safe, as soon as he convinced her to turn the investigation over to a private detective—a detective he would gladly pay for—he would stay away from her. For good this time.

Assailed by spinning lights and squeals of laughter, he circled the spinning cars of the Tilt-a-Whirl and made his way toward the shadowed hulks of the tents devoted to games, selling goods and fortune-telling. The grass between the tents had been worn down by foot traffic, leaving nothing but greasy mud sprinkled with straw. Carnies leaned from the tents hawking games of skill and chance to passersby. Light glowed from a large tent at the end of the row. A sign out front entreated the curious to enter and learn their futures. Garner lifted a corner of the flap and glanced inside.

Amid velvet drapes, silken pillows and candles, an old Gypsy woman hovered over a woman Garner recognized from town. The Gypsy held the woman's hand, tracing the lines of her palm with a withered finger. Gray hair peeked out from under the scarf knotted around her head. Lines deep as mountain gorges creased her face. Gold coin bracelets similar to the earrings Sabina wore tinkled with the movement of her hands. "Understand, my dear, that I see wealth for you. Wealth and success in your career."

The town woman hung on every word.

He let the tent flap fall. Spinning away, he ran smack into a tiny waif of a woman. He grasped her arm, steadying her on her feet. "Pardon me, Miss."

She looked up at him with luminous brown eyes that seemed both childlike and worldly-wise at the same time. She had to be in her mid-twenties, but the way she tilted her head reminded him of a small child with a question. A giggle broke from her lips. "Are you looking for someone?"

"Yes, I am. Do you work here? At the carnival?"

"Work? Sometimes." She giggled again. Her long dark hair curved in wisps with the contour of her neck. Her loose sack of a dress and gold hoops on her ears and wrists made her look like an elf or mischievous pixie of some kind. "I'm Florica."

"Do you know Sabina King, Florica?"

"She's one of the sisters."

He supposed she was referring to Sabina and her sister Alessandra. "Yes. The sisters. She is one of the sisters. Do you know where she is?"

The pixie pointed at the fortune-telling tent. "Valonia is in the tent, not Alessandra. Valonia can't really tell fortunes. Not like Alessandra. Alessandra can see the future. I wonder what she sees now."

Garner looked back at the tent. So the old woman in the tent was the one supposedly cursing everyone. She seemed so small, so frail. She didn't look as if she'd be able to curse her way out of a wet paper bag.

"I'm not looking to have my fortune told. I'm looking for Sabina." He made his words very clear, hoping the young woman would understand.

To his dismay, another giggle bubbled from her lips. "Sabina doesn't tell fortunes. Not like Alessandra."

"I know. I don't want my fortune told. I want to find Sabina."

Now she pointed at a small tent huddled to one side of the tent housing the fortune-teller. "Sabina is a healer. That is her tent."

The tent was dark, the front flap closed and tied. Obviously Sabina wasn't selling her spells. But where was she? He frowned at the sprite. He was getting nowhere here. He'd have to find someone else to help him. Such as Sabina's aunt. He took a step toward the fortune-telling tent.

"Do you need to be healed?"

The pixie's quiet question stopped him in his tracks. He turned back to face her.

"Sabina can heal people. Do you need to be healed?"

He nodded. "Yes. I need Sabina to heal me."

The girl's mouth crooked into a smile. "Then follow me." She whirled and scampered off, her hair and dress fading into the night.

Garner ran to catch up.

She darted in and out of the crowd, passing through pools of shadow and light. As soon as Garner spotted her, she flitted in another direction, her head bobbing as she ran.

He'd trailed her halfway down the alley of games when she disappeared between two game tents. He followed, cutting through the line of tents at the point where he thought she'd vanished. The shadows behind the game booths seemed all the deeper after the swirling lights of the midway and the neon streaming from some of the games. The rotting scent of the day's garbage hung in the air. He scoured the blackness, but the strange, rather fay creature was nowhere to be seen.

In the shadowy field before him, he could make out the hulking shapes of more than a dozen trailers, the traveling homes of the carnival workers. Had Sabina returned to her trailer for the night? Maybe this was where the pixie was leading him before he'd lost her.

Deeply rutted, the field was almost devoid of grass, worn away by feet and tires. He pushed ahead, checking each trailer for light. Through one window, he could see a Gypsy woman tucking children into bed. In front of another trailer, men hunched over guitars, the music drifting on the air and mingling with the calliope and zydeco music of the carnival.

A giggle sounded from behind a trailer to his right. The waif playing a game of hide-and-seek? He rounded the trailer, following the sound. There in the shadows was a pair of teenagers in a clutch. Another giggle rose from the girl's lips.

It was no use. He'd lost Florica. Maybe she'd planned to lead him on a wild-goose chase, he didn't know. With her strange giggle and the impish glint in her eyes, he wouldn't be surprised if she'd played him for her own amusement. Well, if he couldn't find Sabina among the trailers, he would find a ticket seller or someone else on the midway who could help him locate her.

Worry cramped the muscles in his neck and shoulders. What if Sabina wasn't at the carnival? What if something bad had befallen her?

Garner raked a hand through his hair and tried to bring his thoughts under control. No matter where she was, he'd find her. He had to if he wanted to preserve what little bit of peace he had left.

SABINA SAT DOWN among the silk pillows on the bed in her little trailer. Elbows on knees, she cradled her head in her hands. She just didn't have the energy to stand in her tent hawking magic spells to carnival-goers tonight. She was exhausted. Weary to the bone. She'd been running herself ragged trying to scrape up more evidence to support Carlo's case while trying to run both her tent and Alessandra's fortune-telling tent. If it wasn't for Valonia offering to stand in for Alessandra tonight, Sabina didn't know what she would have done.

Drawing a deep breath, she stood, walked the few steps to her little refrigerator and rummaged inside for a cold can of soda. Wyatt's recovery was progressing well. Alessandra planned to return to the carnival tonight. The attorney Garner had asked to take Carlo's case seemed to be doing a good job. Sabina's life would return to normal soon. But somehow that thought didn't bring her relief.

She didn't want her life to return to the way it used to be. She didn't want to travel to the next town, selling her spells, moving through life alone. She wanted change.

She wanted Garner Rousseau.

She shook her head and popped the top of the soda can. She might as well want to be queen.

A thump and scrape sounded outside, rising over the strum of nearby guitars and the music of the carnival. Sabina tensed. Though she was probably being paranoid, she couldn't help remembering the fire that had almost killed Alessandra and Wyatt. She looked around her trailer for something she could use as a weapon. Clutching a wine bottle by the throat, she tiptoed to the door and pushed it open slowly.

A hand closed around her wrist.

Chapter Four

A woman's scream ripped through the humid night.

Garner's heart leaped into his throat. He knew immediately the scream was Sabina's. He could feel it in the pinch of his gut and the shot of adrenaline that slammed into his bloodstream. He raced in the direction of the scream.

Dodging around trailers, he forced his feet to move faster over the rutted terrain. Another scream split the air.

Garner saw her silhouetted in light streaming from the open doorway of a trailer. The outline of a man hulked behind her, one hand holding her around the middle, the other hand on her throat, choking her. He wore a mask, one with a sharp beak and feathers like a bird of prey. The attacker released her throat. He raised his fist and slammed it into Sabina's jaw. Her head snapped back like a doll's, and she slumped to the ground.

A bellow rose in Garner's throat. Finally reaching her trailer, he flung himself at the man. His fist connected with plastic and feathers.

The man spun from Garner's punch. Short yet powerfully built, he regained his balance and lunged at Garner. The blade of a knife flashed in his hand.

Garner grabbed the assailant's forearm and brought it

down hard against the corner of the trailer. The man grunted, but his fist only tightened around the knife's handle. Garner slammed the man's arm against the trailer again. This time a cry of pain broke from under the mask and the fist went slack. The knife hit the dirt and bounced under the shadowed edge of the trailer near where Sabina lay.

Garner held the man with one hand, groping under the trailer's edge with the other. He had to reach that knife first.

Foot lashing out, the man tangled one leg with Garner's and shoved with strong arms. Garner lost his grip on the man's arm and fell backward, hitting the dirt beside Sabina's still form.

The attacker twisted away. He managed to grab the knife. He held it out in front of him, blade flashing in the light from the open trailer door.

On hands and knees, Garner angled his body between the knife and Sabina. The birdman might have the advantage now, but he would never get to Sabina. Garner would make sure of it.

The assailant's head whipped around, as if noticing someone's approach. Taking advantage of the man's distraction, Garner scrambled to his feet and lunged at him, but he wasn't fast enough. The man turned and sprinted away, disappearing into the shadows of the surrounding trailers.

Sabina. He spun back and fell to his knees beside her. She moaned softly, but her eyes remained shut, half-moons of lush lashes brushing pale cheeks.

Fear tinged his mouth, along with the copper flavor of blood. He knelt and gathered her in his arms, then carried her up the few steps and through the open door of the trailer.

The inside looked just like Sabina. Soft, gentle, somewhat exotic. Green pillows lined the bed. Plants of every shape and kind sprang from pots and crept toward the wide windows. Draperies of some shimmery material blocked the night outside.

Sabina stirred in his arms, another moan escaping from her lips. Her eyelids fluttered and opened. Her eyes focused on his, drawing him into their brilliant color, holding on. "Garner?" The word was little more than a breath, but it resonated through him with the force of a shout.

Thank God. She was all right. She wasn't dead. Not like Mary Ann. Not like his mother and father. Sabina was alive and in his arms.

Without thought, he lowered his mouth to hers. Her lips tasted every bit as sweet as he knew they would. Sweet and soft and oh, so responsive.

She put her arms around his shoulders and deepened the kiss, joining her tongue with his. Caressing and tasting and loving.

He reveled in the press of her lips, the scent of her skin, the flavor of her mouth. He wanted to taste all of her, experience all of her, draw her into his soul.

He carried her to the bed and set her down, her head on the silken pillows, without taking his mouth from hers, without breaking the contact. He'd almost lost her. Lost her before he'd really even found her. Before he'd drawn her brilliant color into his soul. Before he could love her.

Love her.

His throat tightened. He pulled his lips from hers and willed his arms to release her.

"You didn't have to stop."

"Yes, I did." He looked down into her eyes, her beautiful, beguiling eyes, and smoothed her hair back from her face with his fingertips. "I'm sorry. I…" He closed his mouth. What could he say? *Sorry, I've had enough loss and regret for a lifetime? I can't risk more by letting myself care about you?*

"I'm sorry, too," she said, offering him a gentle smile, but the sadness in her voice hit him like a well-aimed kick to the gut.

SABINA RAISED her fingers to Garner's face and traced the hard line of his lips. Lips that were so gentle. So tender. Yet so full of tension.

She'd wanted him to kiss her, wanted it with every fiber of her being. But she hadn't wanted this. She hadn't wanted him to be sorry. To torture himself for kissing her. To pull away and leave her empty inside.

He kissed her fingers, then enfolded her hand in his and lowered it to the bed. "I wish things were different."

His wife. His family. The pain of losing them ached in his eyes and in his aura. The fear of caring and losing again. The fear of risk. A fear she knew all too well. She offered him a sad smile. "I know."

He brushed her hair from her cheek, his fingers moving over her jaw.

Even at his gentle touch, her jaw was tender. She sucked in a breath.

He pulled his hand back. "You're going to have one nasty bruise. We need to get some ice on that. Do you have any?"

"I have something better in my tent. A healing balm I make myself. Besides, I heal quickly."

He nodded as if he accepted her answer without question.

A glow of pure warmth and strength infused her. What was it about him that made her feel as if she could do anything each time he looked at her? Each time he accepted her? She felt so strong and safe when he was around. Feelings she had no business experiencing, not when she'd just been attacked right outside her own trailer by a masked man. "Do you think he'll come back?"

Garner shook his head. "Not if he's smart. But we have to call the police and report it. Do you have a phone?"

Now it was her turn to shake her head. "I've never had much need to call anyone, so I've resisted joining the cellphone generation. There's one at the carnival office."

"Do you think you can walk there?"

She sat up and swung her legs over the side of the bed. Although her jaw pounded like someone had taken a sledgehammer to it, the rest of her body seemed to be functioning just fine. Too fine. Sitting next to Garner, her side touching his, she felt heat curl inside her. She tried not to think of the way he'd cradled her in his arms when he'd carried her into the trailer. She tried not to think of the press of his lips on hers, the taste of his mouth, the dance of his tongue. She tried not to think of any of it, but she failed miserably.

A knock sounded on the trailer door. "Sabina?" The voice of a boy teetering on the edge of puberty rang above the jangle of the carnival outside.

Sabina lurched to her feet. Her knees wobbled under her for a moment.

Garner grabbed her arm and held her steady. "Not so fast. I'll get it." He guided her back down to the bed, strode to the trailer door and pulled it open.

"Is Sabina here?"

Garner motioned him into the trailer. "Inside."

It was Peppi, a boy who ran errands for Milo Vasilli, the carnival's owner. When he spotted Sabina on the bed, he dropped his gaze to the floor, cheeks reddening.

"It's okay, Peppi. What has happened? Is your father back?" She'd been looking for Peppi's father, Tony. She needed to ask him a few questions about the directions he'd given when Wyatt had inquired about a public phone. Directions that had resulted in an attempt on Wyatt's life by a knife-wielding assailant.

Peppi shook his head. "He didn't come home again last night. Mama's real worried."

Sabina pressed her lips together. Had something happened to Tony? Or might he have been the one who'd run her and Wyatt off the road? The one who'd attacked her tonight? "I'm sorry to hear he's still not back. If you hear anything, let me know."

"I came to tell you there's a phone call for you at the carnival office. It's Alessandra."

Sabina bolted to her feet, adrenaline shooting through her. Garner reached out and caught her arm. "Wait. You're in no condition…"

She shook her head and tried to pull him with her out the trailer door. "Alessandra was planning to come back to the carnival tonight. She's supposed to be here in an hour. She would only call if it was urgent."

"Well, if you think you're going to go sprinting up to the office, you're wrong. You're going to end up face-down on the midway."

"Then come with me. You can prop me back on my feet."

He shook his head and followed her and Peppi out of the trailer.

Garner by her side and Peppi loping on ahead, Sabina wove through the rows of trailers and broke through the line of carnival games. Crowds shuffled through the narrow alley between game booths. Beyond the games area, the midway was in full swing. Colored lights swirled.

Screams echoed off rides, competing with the sounds of rumbling motors and the jumbled mixture of calliope and zydeco music.

As Sabina, pulse pounding, raced through the crowds with Garner at her side, she tried to imagine why Alessandra had called. Was Wyatt all right? Had the driver of the vehicle that had hit him gone to the hospital to finish the job? Or had Alessandra seen something in one of her visions? The masked man's attack on her? Or something that hadn't happened yet?

She quickened her pace. The carnival office was located where games, midway and trailer lot intersected. Peppi reached it first and opened the door. Sabina and Garner followed him inside.

The trailer was about the size of a food vendor's, the office crammed with a battered desk, mismatched file cabinets and a large safe for the night's receipts, everything Milo needed to keep the carnival running smoothly. A cellular phone perched on the corner of his cluttered desk. Milo had a policy of never allowing the phone to leave the office, for fear it would be lost.

Sabina grabbed it and held it to her ear. "Alessandra?"

"Sabina? Thank God they found you. Are you all right?"

"Fine. I'm fine." Her throat tightened at the fear in her sister's voice. Fear almost palpable even over the phone line. "What happened? What's wrong?"

"I've been having feelings. Bad feelings. About you. About Valonia. Something horrible is going to happen."

"Something? Like what?"

"I don't know. But you're all right?"

"I had some trouble, but I'm fine." There was no point telling Alessandra the details of the attack. It was over. Garner had saved her. She was all right. And besides, chances were, Alessandra had already seen the details in a vision. Or at least some of them. "You mentioned Valonia. What did you see?"

"I saw a letter in Valonia's hand."

"A letter? What kind of letter?"

"I don't know. But I feel Valonia is in great danger. You have to find her. And, Sabina?"

"Yes?"

"Be careful."

"I will. And you'd better stay where you are."

"Don't worry. Wyatt would tie me down before he'd let me walk out the door now."

"Good. I'll call you as soon as I can." Sabina punched the button to end the connection and dropped the phone on the desk.

"What is it?" Concern sharpening his eyes, Garner searched her face.

Sabina grabbed his hand and pulled him toward the door, skirting a file cabinet on her way. "I have to find my aunt." She stepped into the noisy bustle of the midway.

"I saw her when I was looking for you." Garner had to shout to be heard. "She's in the fortune-telling tent."

"Of course. She's filling in for Alessandra." Sabina cut across the midway, the fastest route from the office to Alessandra's tent. Once again she raced through the crowds, this time around the swirling lights of the Tilt-a-Whirl, Garner on her heels.

The fortune-telling tent was dark inside. Quiet. As if it was deserted.

Sabina bit her bottom lip. Reaching the tent's entrance, she threw open the flap and rushed inside. Hands shaking, she groped for matches to light one of the dozens of candles Alessandra used to lend light and atmosphere. Her fingers finally closed over the walnut matchbox. She forced her hands to be steady as she opened the box and struck a match.

The flame sputtered, then glowed. She touched it to the wicks of several candles lining one table. Flickering light suffused the tent, illuminating stacks of silk pillows and gossamer draperies. One table was tipped over, its velvet cloth and candles scattered on the floor. And amid the jumble lay Valonia, her bony fingers clutching a letter.

Chapter Five

"No, no, no..." Anguish and fear tore through Sabina. Her head spun. Her stomach heaved. She fell to her knees and stared at Valonia's still body. There was a gash across her wrinkled brow. The upset table lay near her head, blood on the metal edge, no doubt the spot where her aunt's head must have hit.

Garner stepped past Sabina and knelt close to Valonia. He laid his fingers along her neck, feeling for a pulse. Glancing back to Sabina, he shook his head.

A wail erupted from Sabina's lips. She clamped a hand over her mouth and tried to breathe. She didn't need Garner to say the words. They had already ricocheted through her mind and pierced her heart. Valonia was dead. Sabina couldn't save her. *She was too late.*

"What the hell's going on? Why were you racing across the midway?"

Sabina turned in the direction of the familiar voice.

Tall and strapping, her cousin Andrei stood in the tent's entrance, his face furrowed with concern, his eyes bright with alarm. He focused on Valonia.

Sabina swallowed a sob. She was glad Andrei was here. Though Valonia wasn't related to him by blood, he was part of her carnival family. And except for the time his mother sent him away to school, Andrei had always watched out for his younger cousins. Sabina drew a deep breath and forced her gaze back to Valonia's body.

Andrei rushed forward to Sabina's side. "Can't you do something, Sabina? Can't you help her?"

Sabina shook her head. "She's already dead."

Shock faded from his face and anger took its place. "Who did it?" He zeroed in on Garner.

Sabina shook her head. "We just found her. It was probably the same man who just attacked me. The same one who attacked Wyatt and torched Alessandra's trailer."

"Sweet God." Milo Vasilli pushed the tent flaps aside and stepped into the tent. Face pale, he took in Valonia's body and the wreckage strewn across the floor of the tent. He held the coin he usually flipped in his fingers tightly in his fist. "What has happened here? Burglary?"

"I doubt it," Garner's voice sounded behind Sabina, strong and sure.

Suddenly she had the urge to lean against him the way she had in her trailer after the attack. Lean against him and soak in the strength he seemed to give her so she could face what she needed to face.

Milo ventured farther into the tent, but stopped before he reached Valonia. In Gypsy culture the dead were not to be touched. Their belongings were to be burned or sold off, lest their spirits taint those who came in contact with them. Like Sabina and Andrei, Milo wouldn't go near Valonia's body. Not if he could help it. "I will call the *gadje* police. They will take care of her."

Sabina gave him a grateful smile through the tears she could feel winding down her cheeks. "Thank you, Milo."

He nodded and scurried from the tent.

Sabina looked back down at her aunt. A wail of grief

rose in her throat. She choked it back. She couldn't give in to the sorrow. Not right now. Later she could cry. Later she could mourn. Now she had to concentrate. She had to think.

Through her tears, she focused on the blur of yellowed paper, the envelope still clutched in Valonia's hand. The letter Alessandra had seen in her vision. Doing her best to dash the tears from her eyes with the back of one hand, Sabina leaned closer. An elegant script she didn't recognize graced the front of the envelope. A name.

Carlo.

Her heart went still.

Garner followed her gaze to the letter. His brows rose in question.

"Alessandra saw a letter in my aunt's hand in a vision tonight. It's addressed to Carlo."

"Open it," Andrei urged.

Garner removed the letter from Valonia's hand.

Sabina bent over him, Andrei behind her.

Holding it only by the edges, he untucked the envelope's flap and slid out a piece of yellowed paper. Carefully, he unfolded it and held it so Sabina could read it. Fear pulsed off the handwritten page.

Dearest Carlo—
My husband Richard has found out about us. He's very angry and I fear he's going to do something terrible. Meet me at our place under the spreading oak. Be careful.
No matter what happens, I will always love you.
                                                    Theresa.

"The spreading oak," Sabina murmured. "That huge live oak on the edge of the swamp. That's where Theresa

Granville's body was found ten years ago. That's where she was murdered.'' He excitement mounted. Could this letter be the evidence she was looking for? Evidence that pointed to Theresa's real murderer? Evidence that exonerated her cousin Carlo?

She looked back down at the fluid script. '''My husband Richard has found out about us,''' she read aloud, '''He's very angry.' If *Richard Granville* knew about the affair Theresa was having with Carlo and he knew where she was meeting him, he might have gone there to confront her. *Richard Granville* might have killed his wife.''

Garner folded the letter and slipped it back into it's envelope. ''No wonder my father and now Leon want to keep this under wraps. Richard Granville was a big supporter of my father when he was mayor of Les Baux. And now that he's a state senator, he's an even stronger political ally for Leon.''

Behind Garner, Andrei's face glowed unnaturally pale in the flickering candlelight.

Sabina looked back to the letter in Garner's hand, the letter that might help her prove Carlo's innocence. The letter that Valonia must have been trying to protect when she died. ''So what do we do now? We can't just turn the letter over to the police. What if they cover it up, just like they covered up the bloody fingerprint on Theresa's brooch?''

''Take it,'' Andrei said, his voice tight. ''Take it before the cops get here.''

''That would be withholding evidence in a murder investigation.'' Garner's voice was deadly serious.

''Would it be better to let the *gadje* destroy it?'' A flush of anger replaced the pallor in Andrei's cheeks. ''Would it be better to let them continue to railroad an innocent Gypsy? Let them kill him for a crime he didn't commit?''

Sabina took the letter from Garner's fingers and wrapped it in one of Alessandra's red silk scarves before sliding it into the waistband of her skirt. Her eyes met Garner's. She was about to break the law, the law that he upheld, the law that he practiced every day. Her mouth grew dry as bone.

For a long moment he said nothing, the conflict within him furrowing his brow. Finally he nodded, the movement of his head so slight she couldn't be sure if it was really a movement or just a trick of the flickering candlelight. "We'll make copies and give one to Leon. Maybe this will be enough to convince him he can no longer hide what my father did. Nor can he protect Richard Granville."

Andrei watched Garner, scrutinizing his eyes and the hand that touched Sabina's arm. "Can you get Sabina out of here? Can you make sure she's safe?"

Garner nodded. "Yes."

"Then go. Both of you. I'll take care of the *gadje* police."

AFTER MAKING PHOTOCOPIES of the letter, as well as of the photo of the bloody fingerprint, Garner drove Sabina to his father's home. Now, perched on a packing box in the middle of the kitchen floor, Sabina slipped the six sets of photocopies into six separate envelopes. Her hands were still shaking, making stuffing the envelopes a challenge. And wherever she looked in the nearly empty kitchen, all she could see was Valonia's lifeless face.

She still couldn't believe her aunt was dead. Couldn't believe someone had taken her life tonight. Sabina would miss her terribly. But the worst thing was the knowledge that Valonia would never see Carlo a free man. She would never know that the letter she had found, the one she must have been trying to protect when she died, had helped free her son.

At least Sabina *hoped* the letter would help free Carlo. Judging from the frustrated pitch of Garner's voice coming from his father's office, Leon Thibault was being less than cooperative.

She focused on sealing the last envelope. Garner hadn't told her whom he planned to give the envelopes to, besides Thibault, but she had no doubt Garner had a plan. And that it would work.

He had a way of making her believe everything would work out in the end. Just as being around him made her feel strong and sure of herself, as if she could do anything. As if she was in control of her destiny. As if she could reach out and take anything she wanted. It was a confidence that—growing up as a Gypsy, an outsider—she had never felt before.

She bit her lower lip and set the envelopes on the counter. The only problem was that the more she was around Garner and experienced this feeling he'd planted in her, the more she wanted him. Wanted to sleep in his arms and wake to his kisses. Wanted to laugh with him and share with him and love with him. And not just for tonight, not just for a week or a year, but for always. She wanted to heal his injured heart so he could love again. So he could love *her*.

The door to Garner's father's office slammed shut and Garner's footsteps thunked across the wood floor toward the kitchen. She pivoted to face him as he entered.

His jaw was set at a stubborn angle, and his eyes still burned with anger from the argument she'd overheard.

Sabina braced herself. "What happened? Did he refuse to meet with us?"

"He'll meet with us at the carnival early tomorrow morning."

"Tomorrow? Why not tonight?"

Garner grimaced, lines digging into his forehead and bracketing his mouth. "Because he's busy interrogating your cousin Andrei about your aunt's death. And after I reported the attack on you, he jumped at the opportunity to heap that accusation on Andrei, too."

"Andrei? But he didn't have anything to do with any of it."

"That's what I told Leon. But I think he's more set on following in my father's footsteps and looking for a convenient scapegoat than finding the real murderer. Especially if that murderer could be Richard Granville."

Sabina walked over to Garner on shaky legs. The thought of Andrei being questioned about Valonia's murder as if he was a suspect made her stomach roil. Andrei, her older, handsome cousin, a man with charm to burn, a man she'd looked up to her entire life. "They can't do this. We have to go down there. We have to tell them. We have to get Andrei out of there."

Garner held up a hand to stop her before she could race for the door. "I've taken care of it. I called the attorney who's working with you on Carlo's case. He's on his way to the police station now. They have no sound legal reason to hold Andrei. He'll be out of that interrogation room within the hour."

"You're sure?"

"Oh, yeah. Sometimes the law is the law. Even in Les Baux."

She laid her hand on his chest and looked into his eyes. The rush of power shot through her. It was as if she fed off the look in his eyes. Fed off the way he saw her.

''Thank you. Thank you for doing all this. I don't know what I would do without you.''

The corners of Garner's mouth quirked up, his smile as warm as the Louisiana night. ''You would find another way to save your cousin. You wouldn't give up until you did.''

''Maybe.''

''You would, Sabina. Because you're not a person who gives up. You're a person who needs to help others. And you're strong. Strong enough to overcome any obstacle in your path.''

She wanted to believe him. She wanted to believe the strength came from within her. But she had a sneaking suspicion that he was the real source. She dropped her gaze to the floor and began to shake her head.

Placing his fingers under her chin, he tilted her face so that she was looking at him again. ''You are, Sabina. Trust me.''

Gazing into his eyes, she could almost believe him. ''My sister Alessandra is strong. My aunt was strong. I've never thought of myself as strong.''

''What on earth would make you believe you're not?''

She drew in a breath. She had good reason to believe she wasn't strong. But here with Garner the humiliation, the stifling dependence, the horrible loneliness lost its sting and faded into the past. ''I was married when I was very young. Not yet fifteen.''

Garner's eyebrows shot toward his hairline.

''It's not unusual in Gypsy culture to marry that young. I knew the boy. I liked him. He liked me and needed a wife. And my parents arranged the marriage.''

Lines of concern etched Garner's brow, but he said nothing. He just waited for her to continue.

''His family were very traditional Romany—or as you

call us, Gypsies. When I married, I assumed the role of a traditional Rom wife. I probably could have been happy if we'd had children. I've always loved children. But although there didn't seem to be a physical problem, I never got pregnant. It just wasn't to be.''

"Is that why you're no longer married? Because you didn't have children?''

She shook her head. "When Josephe—Joe's father died, I found out Joe didn't like Rom ways. He had followed the traditions only because his father insisted. Joe wanted the opportunities the *gadje* world could give him. He didn't want to follow Rom ways. And he no longer wanted a Rom wife. I tried to please him by changing, but it was not enough...."

Garner's lips pressed together in a bitter line. "So the bastard ran out on you.''

Sabina shrugged. Joe's leaving had been humiliating. Devastating. But somehow it didn't seem that important anymore. Not when she was standing here with Garner. Not with Garner looking at her this way. "I was fitting myself into the mold of a Rom wife one moment, and the next moment the mold was gone. I guess I've been trying to figure out who I am ever since. If it weren't for Alessandra and my aunt taking me back to the carnival and encouraging me to explore my gifts, I don't know what I would have done.''

"Your gifts. I know you read auras. You have other gifts?''

A shiver of nervousness inched up her spine. Sabina had never talked of this with anyone other than Alessandra, Valonia and Andrei, who all had gifts of their own. Not even Joe had known her power.

Garner watched her, patiently waiting for her answer. Acceptance radiated from his aura. He wouldn't judge her.

He wouldn't be afraid of her powers. He would take whatever she told him in stride.

"I can heal."

His brows slashed low over his eyes. Not in judgment, but seeking to understand. "You mean with the charms you sell at the carnival?"

"No. With my hands." She held her hands out in front of her, palms up. "I can lay my hands on a wound, and if I concentrate hard enough, the wound becomes my own. The person I lay hands on is healed."

"The wound becomes your own?"

"Yes. For a time. It isn't a physical wound you can see, nothing quite so dramatic, but I can feel the pain." She flinched inwardly remembering the pain she endured the last time she healed someone. A long time ago. "My body then heals the wound. Very quickly."

Garner nodded, as if what she told him fell perfectly into place like the missing piece to a puzzle. "That's why Andrei thought you could do something for Valonia. He thought you could heal her. But if you had, and you'd absorbed her wound, wouldn't you have died?"

"Yes. Maybe. I don't really know. I haven't tried to heal more than shallow cuts and bruises. I don't know if I would be able to heal anything more serious. And I don't know what would happen to me if I did."

He nodded. Reaching out, he ran a finger over the palm of her hand. "You're even stronger than I thought. You have a very powerful gift. A powerful purpose."

Yes. Maybe she did. But only if she could learn to use it. If she could learn not to be afraid of it. If she could believe in herself the way Garner believed in her. She laid her hand on his chest again, feeling the steady beat under her palm. "I wish I was strong enough to heal the pain in your heart."

"If I had a fraction of the strength and vitality and love of life that you have, I could heal myself." Tiny lines framed his mouth, and the sadness in his eyes was almost more than she could bear. "But I don't have any strength left, Sabina. And I don't want to hurt you. I couldn't live with hurting you."

GARNER LAY AWAKE, staring at the ceiling of the bedroom he'd slept in as a kid. His heart ached. He'd known Sabina such a short time, but he didn't need to know anything more about her to know he loved her. Loved her with all his heart and soul. Pushing her away tore him up inside. But if he let himself love her, marry her and cherish her the way she deserved, and then he lost her...

He rolled to his side and thumped his pillow with a fist. After they turned the evidence over to Leon tomorrow and mailed the other copies to Carlo's attorney, the attorney general, the governor, the *Les Baux Record* and the *Times-Picayune,* he would turn his father's house over to a Realtor to handle and say goodbye to Sabina for the last time. He would return to St. Louis. And she would travel to the next town with the carnival. And then they would both be safe.

The creak of his bedroom door interrupted his thoughts. He jolted to a sitting position, squinting through the shadows, every muscle tense, ready to fight.

The door swung open, and Sabina slipped inside. Still in her Gypsy skirt and blouse, she glowed like an emerald in the moonlight falling through the window.

"Sabina."

She held a finger to her lips. "Please. Don't say anything. Just hear me out."

He nodded, his heart beating so loudly he was sure she could hear it, too.

"I couldn't sleep. I kept thinking about you and about me and about what is between us." She paused, as if searching for the words to go on, the words to describe what couldn't be described.

Garner sat up and swung his legs over the side of the bed. Sitting on the edge, he said nothing, as he'd promised. He just watched her, soaked her in.

She took a deep breath, as if drawing strength. "I know we don't have a future. But I also know we can't waste what we do have. It's too rare. Too precious."

Now it was his turn to draw strength. What she said was true. Every word spoke to the longing in his soul. "But—"

She held up a hand, stopping his protest. "I need you, Garner. I need your arms around me." Even in the moonlight he could see her body tremble. With need. With want.

Just as his own body trembled.

"I don't want our memories of each other to be filled only with regret, Garner. I want to remember the feel of your skin on mine. Your hands touching me."

Arousal pulsed inside him like an undeniable force. A need only she could satisfy. Night after night of loneliness stretched in front of him. Nights when he would have nothing more than the memory of her softness, her scent, her loving to pull him through.

"Please, Garner. Don't throw away what is so good, so rare. Give us something to remember. Give us tonight."

He stood up and crossed to her. He couldn't refuse. He couldn't even think. He didn't want to. He wanted only one thing. Sabina. Raising his hand, he traced a finger down the silken skin of her cheek.

She peeled the soft, gauzy top over her head. She wasn't wearing a bra, and her breasts hung free, breath-

taking in the moonlight. She lowered her arms and
dropped the top to the floor. Her necklace glinted from
where it rested just above her breasts.

He reached out a hand, teasing first one nipple and then
the other with his fingers until they puckered, hard and
ready for the attention of his mouth.

Give us tonight, she'd said.

He'd do his best. For her and for himself. Because after
tonight, memories would be all they had.

He lowered his lips to one breast. Littering kisses over
the supple mound, he circled her nipple before taking it
into his mouth. He suckled and nipped, reveling in the
arch of her body and the moan of pleasure from her lips.

She reached her arms around him, trailing her fingers
down his back. Goose bumps rose on his skin at her touch.
Her hands found the waistband of his briefs and inched
the elastic down over his buttocks. The briefs caught on
his erection. She followed the waistband with her fingers
until her hands were between their bodies. She slipped the
stubborn briefs over his hardness and down his legs. Once
they were out of the way, she cupped him with her warm
hands and stroked his length.

He gasped at the caress of her fingers and the soft tickle
of her gauzy skirt on his skin. Abandoning her breasts for
a moment, he lowered himself to his knees in front of her.
Hooking his fingers in the waistband of her skirt, he
inched it down over the curve of her hips. He caught her
panties in his fingers, as well, pulling them down with the
skirt until he exposed the triangle of soft hair nestled between her thighs.

He brought his mouth to her, kissing, caressing until
she cried out in need. Until his hunger grew so acute, he
feared he couldn't hold out much longer.

Standing, he led her to the bed and laid her down on

it. Leaning over her, he lowered his mouth to kiss her breast.

She pulled him down to her. "Please, Garner. I want you. I need you now." She wrapped her legs around him and drew him close.

He covered her mouth with a kiss. Expelling a shuddering breath, he eased inside her.

They moved as one, sensation, passion building with each thrust. Until she shattered beneath him. Until he couldn't hold out anymore and he joined her in release. Until their sweat-slick bodies collapsed together on the sheets.

"Oh, it's so beautiful."

He nuzzled the shell of her ear. "What?"

"Our auras are touching and mingling. A kaleidoscope of color. I've never seen anything like it before."

He had to agree. As ridiculous as it sounded, he was sure nothing this dazzling, this earthshaking, had ever happened before. Not to anyone. And certainly not to him. He felt infused by color. Alive with color.

Without pulling away, he raised himself on his elbows and peered into her lovely face. "Yes. It was beautiful."

"Did you see it?"

"I can see it in your eyes."

They made love throughout the night, until they were both so exhausted, all they wanted was to sleep in each other's arms. And after Sabina drifted off to sleep, Garner stayed awake, still nestled in her warmth. Still part of her. Until the sun inched its way over the horizon and its rays glowed through the dusty windows. He couldn't let go, couldn't give her up. Because once he did, she would be gone forever. Once he did, all that he would have would be memories.

Chapter Six

"I know who you're looking for, and I know where he is."

Sabina narrowed her eyes on Florica Vasilli. She and Garner had been waiting at the carnival office for Leon Thibault to arrive for more than twenty minutes, and despite his promises to show, he was nowhere in sight. "Where is he, Florica?"

"He went to the fun house. The fun house. The fun, fun, fun house." The girl swayed back and forth to the strains of zydeco coming from the office radio as she chanted the words, an ethereal smile curving her lips.

Sabina drew in a deep breath, striving for patience. She'd never been able to figure Florica out. Although the woman was only a few years younger than Sabina, she had the innocence and demeanor of a child. Even her aura was that of a child. A rainbow of color. Unspoiled. Unmarred. And also quite unreadable.

Garner stepped closer to Florica. "The fun house? Why is he in the fun house?"

Florica's smile grew so wide her entire face was transformed into a mask of mischief. "That's where I saw him go." A musical giggle bubbled from her lips.

Garner frowned.

Sabina reached for his hand, lacing her fingers with his.

He looked at her, the bittersweet expression shadowing his eyes a reflection of her soul. Last night had been more than she'd ever dreamed. Ever hoped. Garner was a wonderful lover. Passionate, considerate, just as she knew he would be. But it was the way their auras had touched that still had her senses reeling.

And left her with a hole in her heart.

She pushed away the thought. She couldn't focus on what it would be like when Garner was gone. This morning he'd told her of his plans to leave immediately following their meeting with Leon Thibault. She only had a few hours left with him. A few hours to touch his hand, to lace her fingers with his. And she wouldn't waste it. Not one second.

But she couldn't concentrate on that now. Now they had to find Leon Thibault.

Sabina narrowed her eyes and gave Florica a gentle but firm smile. Judging from Florica's mischievous giggle, Sabina wouldn't be surprised if she'd directed Thibault to the fun house herself as a prank. "We'll go look for District Attorney Thibault at the fun house, then, Florica. But if we miss him and he comes back to the carnival office, I want you to tell him to stay put. Do you hear me?"

Florica shifted her weight from one foot to another. "Do you hear me?" she mocked in a schoolmarm's tone, then broke into giggles that looped and danced in the already steamy morning air.

Garner turned to Sabina and shook his head. "Let's go to the fun house. If we miss him, we'll track him down ourselves."

FINGERS TIGHTENING around the ivory handle of his knife, he pushed open the door of the fun house and let himself

inside. He'd seen how Sabina had narrowed her eyes at
Florica. Just as he'd heard her pressing Florica for information, all the while watching and assessing. Sabina King
had powers. Powers he didn't understand. Powers that
frightened him.

He pulled the blade from its sheath and ran his thumb
across the edge. Razor sharp and ready. Just as he always
kept it. He'd tried to warn Sabina away from digging
where she didn't belong. God knows he'd tried. Just as
he'd warned her sister and Wyatt Boudreaux. Just as he'd
tried to warn the old woman.

Guilt plunged into his heart.

He hadn't planned to kill the old woman. That had been
unfortunate. But it couldn't be helped. She'd put it all
together. She was going to tell.

And he couldn't let her tell.

She'd tried to get away from him, knocking over a table
in her haste, scattering candles and velvet across the rugs.
He'd had no choice but to grab her, to pound her head
against the table's steel edge until her life slipped away.
Just as he'd had no choice when he'd tried to kill Alessandra and Wyatt with the fire and tried to run down Wyatt Boudreaux with the rental car.

And he had no choice now but to kill Sabina King and
Garner Rousseau.

He'd do whatever he had to. And this time he wouldn't
fail.

SABINA USUALLY LOVED mornings at the carnival. The
freshness of the air. The quiet before the activities kicked
into full gear. But this morning was different. This morning, the air seemed to carry a clammy chill despite the
already building heat. And the quiet set her nerves
on edge.

The fun-house entrance yawned in front of them, a large painted mouth framed with sharp teeth and bright red lips. Later in the day, it would be filled with children and their parents laughing at their distorted images in the mirrors, trying to find their way through the dark mazes, shrieking with fear when the unexpected popped out at them from behind a wall. But now it was silent except for the sound of Sabina and Garner's footsteps on the wooden ramp.

"Leon?" Garner shouted. "Are you in there?"

A muffled thump and a curse filtered through the fun-house walls.

Garner chuckled and shook his head. "I'll bet Florica told Leon to wait for us here."

"I thought the same thing. It's just her style."

"She must think we *gadje* are a gullible lot. First she led me on a chase last night. And now she has Leon lost in the fun-house maze."

Sabina paused. "Maybe we should make him promise to consider our evidence before we let him out."

Garner gave her a smile. "Not a bad idea." He pushed at the center of the huge lolling tongue and the mouth squeaked open.

Sabina followed him through the frame of teeth and lips. The maze was dark. Lights flashed ahead, illuminating moving eyes and wicked clown faces that watched from the shadows. Sabina and Garner approached the hall of mirrors, an attraction no good fun house was without. Mirrors of all shapes and sizes loomed around them. Sabina watched their distorted images move through the hall. Short and fat, thin and tall, and serpentine, but always hand in hand, together. For now, together.

A creak of floorboards caught her ear. She glanced in the direction of the sound.

A blur of movement emerged from the darkness. Dark feathers. A hawklike beak. Fingers as strong as talons dug into her arm with bruising force. A flash of steel came out of the darkness, swooping toward her. A scream erupted from her throat.

Garner spun around. He grabbed the hand with the knife, stopping its downward assault.

The birdman slammed him back against a mirror. The glass splintered and broke, showering to the floor.

Garner's grip slipped.

The birdman wrenched his wrist free. He jabbed the blade at Garner.

No!

Sabina rushed the man. Leaping on his back, she grasped his throat with one hand and clawed at his face with the other, trying to gouge her fingers through the holes in the mask and into his eyes.

Garner lunged at the man at the same time. The attacker pushed Garner back into another mirror. His fist shot toward Garner's stomach. *The fist gripping the knife.*

Please, God, no.

Garner stood still for a moment, staggering against the mirror, leaning against it. A red stain began to spread down his shirt. Blood.

The man rushed backward, driving Sabina into another mirror.

Air exploded from her lungs. Glass shattered behind her. She released his throat and fell from his back, gasping for breath. Just then a voice yelled from outside the fun house. Andrei. She could swear the voice belonged to Andrei. "Andrei!" she screamed.

The birdman leaped over Garner and thundered down the fun-house hallway, disappearing into the maze.

Sabina scrambled to Garner's side. Shards of glass from

the broken mirror cut her hands and knees. She clawed at his shirt, ripping the fabric wide to expose his wound. A deep gash slashed across his stomach, blood pulsing from it.

She looked into Garner's face. His pale, strong face. His eyes were already growing glassy, unseeing. His breath shuddered from his lips. Darkness surrounded him. The black aura of death.

Oh, God, Garner was going to die.

Sabina leaned him back against a mirror and held her hands up in front of her. Her fingers stretched out, steady and strong. Garner couldn't die. He couldn't. Whatever it took, she'd save him. She would, because she was strong. Powerful. And she didn't want to live without the man she loved.

She pressed her palms to his wound. Blood oozed between her fingers, hot and sticky.

Garner's eyes widened. Understanding dawned in his glassy eyes. "No. Sabina, no." He clawed at her hands with his fingers. He tried to push her away, but his strength had drained away, along with his blood.

She pressed her hands harder against his wound. "I love you, Garner. Always remember I love you."

Slowly the blood flow lessened, then stopped. She could feel his cut flesh coming together, mending under her fingers. Just as pain ripped into her own flesh, and it seemed as if her blouse was wet with blood.

Strength seemed to pour out of her with each beat of her heart. She gasped, the roar of breath deafening in her ears. Raising her eyes, she looked at her own distorted image in the mirror. Her eyes grew sunken, her cheeks drained of color, of life.

And all around her hung the black aura of death.

Chapter Seven

Garner fought through the fog in his mind as if waking from a horrible dream. Sabina. He had to reach Sabina. He had to stop her. He forced his eyes to focus.

Sabina was crouched next to him in the narrow hall of mirrors. Shards of broken glass glinted all around her. Her fingers pressed his stomach, cold against his skin. She stared past him and into the mirror behind him. Her breathing rasped in the silence, fast and shallow.

A chill penetrated his bones and froze his heart.

She'd saved him. She'd healed him. She'd placed her hands on him and absorbed his wound, just as she'd described.

And now she was going to die.

"No." The word exploded from Garner's lips again, from his heart, from his soul. She couldn't die. She couldn't. He loved her.

Just as he'd loved Mary Ann. Just as he'd loved his mother and even in some strange way, his father.

Love is death.

Sabina would die because he loved her. She was right. That was his curse. *Love is death.*

He gathered her in his arms. She slumped against his shoulder, as if she didn't have the strength to hold her body upright one more second. He tilted her face toward his, and latched on to her gaze. What he wouldn't give to lose himself in the rich green of her eyes, to plunge in over his head, without a life vest, without a safety line, just plunge in and let the tide sweep him away.

She'd been right when she'd said what they had was rare and precious. Too precious to waste. And what had he done? He'd wasted it. All because he was too busy protecting his heart until it was too late.

No. It wasn't too late. It damn well wasn't too late. He wouldn't let it be. "You're not going to die, Sabina. I'm not going to let you."

She looked up at him, her eyes unseeing.

His gut twisted with anger. "Damn it, Sabina. You can't die on me now. I love you. I want you here with me."

The corners of her lips quirked upward, as if she'd heard him. As if she'd tried to smile. She drew a deep, shuddering breath.

"You're strong, Sabina. Strong enough to heal yourself. Strong enough to come back to me." He drew her close and held her tightly against his shoulder. "Damn it, come back to me."

He heard mirror shards crunch underfoot. Looking up, he met the eyes of Sabina's cousin. Andrei seemed to take in the situation with a glance, his eyes rounding with fear for his cousin. He didn't rush forward, though, but stayed in the shadows. As if he understood that he couldn't help. That only Garner could save Sabina now.

Garner kissed Sabina's hair and held her tighter against his body. "I want to marry you. I want us to have children. You said you loved children. We can have as many as you want. And I want all of them to be filled with your strength and zest for life. I want all of them to be just like you.''

She stirred in his arms, but he didn't let her go. He couldn't.

''But you have to come back to me first, Sabina. You have to heal yourself. You can do it. I know you can. You're the strongest person I've ever known.''

''You make me strong.''

Her voice was weak as a whisper, but it hit him with the force of trumpet fanfare. He loosened his embrace so he could see into her eyes.

Dark, rich green stared back at him. The color of life itself.

He swallowed into an aching throat. ''You're strong, Sabina. You always have been. You just didn't know it.''

A smile flitted over her lips. ''I'm glad you were around to let me in on the secret.'' Her voice was still weak, but gaining strength with each word.

''You're strong enough to heal yourself. You're strong enough to come back to me.'' He hadn't asked a question, but still he waited for her answer. A few moments ago he wouldn't have dared hope for a miracle like this. Now he couldn't stop hoping.

She nodded. ''Help me sit up so I can see myself in the mirror.''

''Your aura?''

''Yes.''

He did as she asked.

She stared at her reflection a long time in silence.

''What do you see?'' He held his breath.

Finally she turned to face him, sitting upright under her own power. ''I see love. The clear, pink color of love.''

Tears blurred his vision. Tears of relief. Tears of hope.

"Yes. I think I can see it, too." And he could. If not in the air surrounding them, then in his heart. In his soul.

All the brilliant colors of life sparkled and danced in her eyes. "My aunt's curse is broken. You love me, and yet I didn't die."

He slipped his fingers over her cheeks and into her hair, cradling her face in both hands. The curse was broken. But there was more than that. So much more. He wanted to tell her about the rush of joy that made his head spin. The hope that filled his heart to bursting. The love that touched his soul. But the words wouldn't form on his tongue. All his life, words had been his tools. Tools to defend the meek. Tools to fight back against his father. Tools to protect himself against pain and loss. But now, for the first time, words failed him. Because he didn't need them now.

He traced his thumbs along her cheekbones. Leaning down, he fitted his lips to hers. And when he finally found the strength to pull away, he looked deep into the green of her eyes and found his peace.

ANDREI
PATRICIA ROSEMOOR

Thanks to my agent Jenn Jackson,
for all her hard work in my behalf.

Chapter One

A throwback to days past, Granville Plantation set the standard against which other such estates were compared. Framed by live oaks, the mansion dripped with Louisiana character. Strong white pillars. Welcoming front porch. Charming landscaping. Tall, wide windows like the eyes of a living being gazing out on the world haughtily, as if certain of its own superiority.

Just like its owner, Andrei Sobatka remembered ruefully.

He was staring at the best of bayou country and stewing about the past when the front door opened, jolting him out of a memory better off forgotten.

A woman stepped onto the porch, a tall glass in one hand, and leaned a slender shoulder into one of the columns. She looked out at the land with the possessiveness of a lifelong lover. Wearing tan riding pants, black boots and a bright white shirt open at the throat, she was a study in equestrian elegance. She'd surely been riding—her boots were mud-spackled and her shirt, stained with sweat, clung to her like a second skin. Seeming satisfied with her own narrow world, she raised the glass to her lips, her chin lifting to reveal a long, elegant neck as she sipped at her drink.

She hadn't changed, Andrei thought, moving closer, mesmerized by the golden locks of hair plastered along her neck. He hadn't seen her since the last summer he'd worked with the carnival ten years before, but it might just as well have been ten days.

For a moment he was caught, lost in the fantasy of trailing his fingers through those silky strands, of brushing them back from her warm flesh, of running his mouth along the alabaster column of her neck and drinking her in.

Suddenly he realized she'd looked straight through the trees and noticed him. The color in her cheeks rose, and as he drew closer, he could see the pulse in her throat. Her heart was hammering, he thought, rushing aristocratic blue blood through her delicate veins. She clutched the glass as she might a lifeline, and he could see she wore no wedding ring.

"What are you doing on Granville property?" she demanded.

"Now, Lizzie," he drawled, purposefully emphasizing the nickname, "is that any way to say hello after all these years?"

"I would rather say nothing at all to you, but since you're trespassing, you leave me no choice. And don't call me by that wretched name. It's Elizabeth."

He moved closer still, stopping inches from the step. "You used to love it when I called you Lizzie."

"I *allowed* you to call me Lizzie."

That haughty tone sparked memories. Her voice as smooth and sleek as her long legs and high breasts had haunted his dreams for years after the last time he'd seen her.

He laughed. "You loved it when I called you Lizzie.

And when I trespassed on sacred Granville land, if I remember correctly, it was because you invited me.''

"So I was young and foolish. A teenager," she added as if that should explain it all. "I'm a woman now."

He eyed her with the lust of a connoisseur, his gaze intimately brushing her breasts. The areolas were large enough and dark enough to show just slightly through her thin bra and damp shirt. "You certainly are a woman."

Her nipples pebbled visibly through her thin shirt, and Andrei felt a surge from below in answer.

"A different person," she emphasized, crossing her arms before her as if she needed to protect herself from his gaze.

He shook his head. "You're the same as I remember you."

Liquid spilled from her glass. Flustered, she set it down on a nearby porch table.

Softly, he taunted her. "I could make you like my calling you Lizzie again."

"Never."

She was a little breathless and he was so close he could see the perspiration dotting her skin, making her look all dewy and soft, like a woman who'd just been made love to. The thought plagued him, filled him with a lust she would never know.

"I could make you beg me to take you, not in a bed with nice clean sheets, but out in a pasture or deep in the heart of bayou country—"

"Stop it! Why have you come back here, Andrei? What is it you want?"

An easy grin tugged at his lips. "And if I said *you?*"

"I would call you a liar." Her jaw tightened and she added, "A Gypsy."

As if the words were interchangeable, Andrei thought,

quick anger slashing through him. He narrowed his gaze on Elizabeth Granville and took the two steps up to the porch. Something flashed through her expression—fear?—and he knew the advantage was his.

"To be Rom does not automatically make one a liar." His tone lacked its former come-on. He was all straight arrow now, no more nonsense. "I'm looking for your father."

"Daddy? Why?"

"We have business."

"What kind of business?"

"As a state senator, he represents me, doesn't he?" Andrei said this as if that was all the reason he needed.

"I work for Daddy. Whatever the business, you can tell me and I'll see that it's taken care of."

"You'll take care of *me?*" he asked, grinning at her again just to throw her off balance.

"I can see this conversation is going nowhere." Abruptly she turned and headed for the door.

"Tell me where your father has slithered off to and I'll leave you be."

Her spine stiffened. She turned back and gaped. "Excuse me?"

"A simple request. What rock did he crawl under?"

"You're calling Daddy a snake?"

"That would be an insult to snakes."

"How dare you!"

"I call them like I see them."

"You haven't seen Daddy in almost a decade, so what do you have against him? His politics?"

"If that's what you want to call it. I don't like that he's walking around free while Carlo Mustov is still sitting on death row."

Because he believed that no Romany would ever get a

break from the law, Andrei had tried to stay out of the investigation. But now Valonia had been murdered, and his beloved cousins Alessandra and Sabina had both put their lives on the line. Too bad their sacrifices had come to naught—they still hadn't achieved the result they all wanted, which was to free Carlo.

After a stunned silence, she asked, "Would you care to explain that?"

"You don't think your father is capable of murder?" He could see that she didn't.

"Whom do you imagine he killed?"

"Your mother, Lizzie," he said, watching her amber eyes go round with shock. "Thankfully, he failed when he tried to kill Garner Rousseau."

Andrei had chased away the would-be murderer but hadn't caught the bastard. As he'd expected, District Attorney Leon Thibault had not been overly excited by the letter Sabina had handed him when the whole frightening episode in the fun house was over. The D.A. had been searching for Sabina and Garner at the opposite ends of the midway. Florica must have been confused, but then, Andrei knew better than to rely on the childlike woman he had befriended upon returning to the carnival.

Lizzie's incredulous "You're out of your mind!" brought him out of his musings.

"Am I?"

"Absolutely!"

Perhaps he was, for after witnessing Sabina's selflessness in healing Garner, he'd been shamed into taking action at last. Sabina and Garner were safely on their way to Baton Rouge to check out Richard Granville's story— that Lizzie's father had gone on government business there late on the night of the murder—so investigating closer to home was, for the moment, his responsibility alone.

"There's no finer Southern gentleman than Daddy," Lizzie told him.

"Are you saying that a Southern gentleman can't also be a murderer?"

"Not if you're talking about my father."

"You wouldn't be a little shortsighted, now would you?"

"Go to hell, Andrei Sobatka!"

"Too late. I already have an intimate acquaintance with the place."

She turned and again tried to escape, but he grabbed her forearm and swung her back against a column. As fast as he'd ever moved, he slashed her arms up above her head and pinned them there, his long fingers gripping her delicate wrists. He could feel her pulse race. Then he pinned her body to the pillar with his.

"What the hell do you think you're doing?" she asked with a gasp.

What was he doing? Most likely being a fool. He couldn't help himself. Apparently she was having the same problem, for he sensed need trembling through her, saw deep into her darkening amber gaze where desire for him smoldered. He knew what women wanted—Gypsy magic, Lizzie would call it—and it was both a blessing and a curse. Nothing could come of such torture, not anymore, but memory plagued him and for a moment he allowed himself the fantasy.

Dipping his head toward her hair, he inhaled her scent, as rich and ripe as Mother Earth, a combination of magnolia soap and fine leather and horseflesh. He remembered that combination of scents. Remembered more. Considering the way she froze, the way her breath came in little catches, he suspected she remembered, as well.

Miss Elizabeth Granville, debutante, was held fast to the spot, licking her lips, as nervous as a cat. He almost gave way to temptation and licked them, too.

Almost.

With a sardonic laugh, he backed off and saluted her. "Tell your daddy that Andrei Sobatka is looking for him."

She said nothing, merely stared at him as he leaped off the porch, not even touching the stairs. He felt her gaze on his back as he swiftly moved off. The sensation never left him, not until he disappeared from sight and made his way back through the bayou and across the road to the carnival grounds.

Chapter Two

No doubt about it, Andrei Sobatka was a heartbreaker and always had been, Elizabeth knew. Coming back here to the carnival was so difficult, more difficult than she'd thought. Mentally arming herself against the man's charms, she stepped foot on the carnival grounds for the first time in almost a decade.

Familiar sights and sounds—guys hawking rides and games, the smell of popcorn and funnel cake—brought her back to old times. She'd always been attracted to this colorful disarray so at odds with her own ordered life. As an only child who'd suffocated from her parents' sheltering, she'd wondered what it would be like to be so free...and one summer she had found out.

But the past was the past, Elizabeth reminded herself as she caught sight of a Gypsy girl in long skirts and jingling bracelets. Gliding toward the trailers and humming to herself, the girl seemed lost in her own world.

"Excuse me," Elizabeth said. "Can you tell me where I can find Andrei Sobatka?"

The girl jerked around, her dark hair swinging along her shoulders. Not a girl, but a woman, slender and fey, who gave Elizabeth the once-over, then arched pencil-thin eyebrows at her business suit and high-necked blouse. Smothering a giggle, she said, "He's working of course."

Knowing she was overdressed for the occasion—a self-defense way of putting herself in the superior position—Elizabeth asked, "Where?"

For a moment she didn't think the young woman would answer her, then wondered if she was waiting to be tipped for the information. The odd way the Gypsy was staring at her…

But before Elizabeth could put a hand to her shoulder bag, the Gypsy smothered another giggle and said, "Tilt-a-Whirl."

Before her thank-you was out of her mouth, the girl had disappeared. Shrugging, Elizabeth headed in the direction of the rides.

And then she saw him. Andrei. Dark hair swathed his rugged bronzed features—high forehead, well-defined cheekbones, square chin softened by a slight indentation. She remembered once exploring that shallow cleft with a fingertip, remembered the way he'd trapped her hand to suck on…

With a sharply indrawn breath, Elizabeth pushed the memory back to the purgatory where it belonged.

Even from a distance, she responded to Andrei's easy smile and sultry good looks. This morning he was using them on three high-school girls, who seemed unable to make up their minds about trying out his ride.

"Get your tickets, lovely ladies," he drawled. He seemed distracted for a moment—had he spotted her? Elizabeth wondered—then quickly went on, "I promise, I'll give the best ride in southern Louisiana just for you."

"But it'll mess up my hair," one of the girls complained as she shot an annoyed look at the knot of boys standing in line for tickets.

"Real men like messy hair," Andrei told her. "And they especially like girls who aren't afraid to be bold."

Though Andrei hadn't looked directly at her, Elizabeth knew he was aware of her presence—she figured the last comment had been meant for *her* ears. He had a way with women of all ages. Seeming to know what they wanted to hear, he gave it to them. The girl didn't know that. Obviously flattered, the teenager whispered to her friends, and, laughing, they headed straight for the ticket booth lineup.

Elizabeth stood her ground and watched Andrei pretend she wasn't there as he stopped the ride and kept his dark gaze pinned to the people exiting.

How dare he show up at her doorstep to accuse her father of her mother's murder and then when she pays him a return visit, ignore her!

"All aboard," Andrei called, finally swinging his gaze to Elizabeth as if challenging her right to be there.

Behind him, the girls were clambering into the last vacant car of the ride. The one he'd talked to was primping, fussing with her hair, no doubt enchanted by him.

Remembering how Andrei had enchanted *her* into a night she would never forget, Elizabeth pitied the foolish girl.

She watched him check the safety bar of each car to make certain it was secure. Even with his back to her, she felt a strong pull to the broad shoulders revealed by a sleeveless T-shirt and the tight buttocks caressed by a pair of jeans. He was a beautiful male specimen, she admitted, even more beautiful than he'd been as a teenager.

He was also more arrogant, if that was possible, as evidenced by his knowing look aimed at her before he started the ride. Surely he didn't think her visit was personal.

Suspecting he did, Elizabeth fumed.

For years, she'd fantasized about Andrei returning— worse, she'd longed to hear a declaration of love when he did. But fantasies were for teenagers, she thought, glancing at the girls on the ride, who shrieked with glee as their car seemed to jerk and spin harder and faster than the others.

Puzzled, Elizabeth wondered whether Andrei had done something to make the ride more thrilling for them alone.

Watching more closely, she suddenly became aware that she, in turn, was being watched. Meeting Andrei's bold gaze, she felt as young and inexperienced as one of the screaming girls. He looked away first and ended the ride, and Elizabeth forced herself to remain where she was.

While the teenagers scrambled out of the cars, Andrei signaled to a young worker, who jogged up and took over the controls.

Then Andrei strolled straight for her and indicated they should move away from the ride. She followed him until the delighted screams grew faint. He stopped at the rear of the fun house. Now aware that this is where Garner Rousseau had been attacked, she grew a bit nervous. Such an odd choice, as if Andrei wanted to keep her on edge.

"So why are you here, Lizzie?" he asked in that slow, syrupy way of his that made her flush all over.

She stared into his eyes, dark as ever, but now shadowed with something she hadn't seen before. Secrets? She shifted and blinked.

"I want Mama's murderer to pay for his crime."

"As do we all."

"But that wouldn't be Daddy. I believe with all my heart that he is innocent. Can you say the same about Carlo?"

"The facts speak for themselves. Everyone who has tried to clear Carlo's name has either ended up dead or been targeted for murder. Plus, there's a photograph of your mother's brooch with a bloody fingerprint on it."

"I don't remember anything about a fingerprint."

"Exactly."

A chill shot through her. "Indeed, that's all troubling. But it doesn't make *Daddy* guilty."

"Your mother was cheating on him—that gives him motive."

She winced. "We don't even know that he was aware of Mama's affair before..."

Before she'd been murdered, Elizabeth didn't have to say. Though it was likely, she admitted silently. The echoes of heated words between her parents haunted her. They'd argued, in fact, on the very evening Mama had been murdered, before Daddy had taken off for Baton Rouge.

"Actually he *did* know." Andrei slipped a folded piece of paper from his pocket. "I think you'd better read this."

She backed away. "What is it?"

"A letter from your mother to Carlo. It's a copy. We found the real thing when we found Valonia's body—she was holding it in her hand."

Elizabeth licked her lips and took the copy from him. She scanned the missive—yes, it was Mama's handwriting. She'd seen it often enough, every time she went through her scrapbook, which she did often so she wouldn't forget her mother.

...my husband Richard has found out about us. He's very angry and I fear he's going to do something terrible...

Feeling faint, Elizabeth took a deep breath and gathered every ounce of Granville starch she could muster.

Shoving the offending letter back at him, she said, "This doesn't prove anything."

Andrei's expression was disbelieving. "What is it going to take to convince you, Lizzie?"

"That my father is a murderer? Proof positive."

"There's definite proof of evidence tampering."

"Anything that points to Daddy?"

"No, not exactly."

Elizabeth closed her eyes and took a deep breath. "Well, then."

Andrei's "Though he was a friend of the D.A. at the time" shook her relief a tad.

"Claude Rousseau had a lot of friends," she insisted. "He was a politician. That didn't mean he would overlook a murder."

Andrei shrugged. "Okay, then other than Carlo or your father, who else might have had a motive to kill your mother?"

"Everyone loved Mama." She shook her head. She would not believe her father had anything to do with her mother's murder. She *wouldn't!* "No one."

"Someone did."

"Then we need to find out who."

"Did your mother ever have a problem with anyone in Les Baux?" Andrei asked. "Or more to the point, did one of the upstanding citizens have have a problem with her for some reason?"

"Not that I remember." At least he was willing to consider there could be another suspect, Elizabeth thought.

"You need to learn for certain. Talk to her friends, find out if they were aware of any disagreements, no matter how petty."

Elizabeth thought about it for a moment. "If anyone would know, Miss Ina would. She's the town's social maven. Or was. She's getting on in years now, and she doesn't get out unless someone accompanies her, but her mind is still sharp, and she has always had her finger on the pulse of the town. If someone from Les Baux has something to hide, I would bet Miss Ina knows about it.''

''She sounds like a good place to start.''

''I can probably catch her this afternoon. And you'll quiz your colleagues here at the carnival?'' Elizabeth asked, growing warm when Andrei arched an eyebrow, no doubt at her formal wording. Trying not to appear flustered, she went on, ''It could be one of them, as well, even if it isn't Carlo. Or do the same people work here who did ten years ago?''

''A few.''

Andrei's visage darkened, no doubt at her intimation that another Gypsy might still be responsible. ''Hopefully someone here has a long memory, as well.''

''Your mother, to start,'' Elizabeth said. ''She was the prosecutor's chief witness, after all.''

''My mother is no longer with the carnival. After my father died several years ago, she had no reason to stay.''

''Oh.''

''But of course I will call her, though I doubt that her story will have changed.''

''Which you should carefully consider,'' Elizabeth murmured.

''You're calling my mother a liar?''

Elizabeth's brows shot up. After all, he'd called her father a murderer and a snake. ''Just the opposite.''

''Then you're saying my mother couldn't be a liar because she's a *gadji* like you.''

''I don't make those distinctions.''

''You made one about me yesterday.''

Having accused him of being a liar and equating that

with Gypsy, Elizabeth was ashamed of herself. She stared down at a spot on the ground. "I was angry, and I apologize. Now, about your mother—"

"You know she didn't see anything, right?"

"I know she overheard an argument between Mama and Carlo," Elizabeth said.

It seemed Mama had been arguing with everyone in her life that day, even her, Elizabeth remembered. That argument had been about the man standing before her. He'd been just a boy then, of course, and it hadn't made sense to Elizabeth that Mama had wanted her to stay away from him. And in light of the ensuing circumstances, it made even less sense—unless Mama had suspected they were both in danger.

Elizabeth went on, "Maybe she'll remember more than Mama trying to break it off with Carlo."

"Such as?"

"A name. Someone who knew about them. Perhaps the person who went to Daddy? That person might have had an ulterior motive."

"You're taking this seriously."

"Of course I am." That letter was damning—she would do anything to clear her father' name.

"I didn't expect it of you."

"Maybe there's more to me than you think." She held out her hand to shake. "It's a deal, then, right? We work together to find the real murderer. Even if it still turns out to be Carlo?"

"Even if it turns out to be your father?"

"It won't."

Only after he took her hand, after he traced the lines of her palm with his thumb, which made her begin to shake deep inside, did he ask, "Are you willing to take a blood oath?"

The tension building in her multiplied. "Blood oath?"

"That what we learn we share? No protecting anyone."

"I'm willing to share information. The blood part...not so much."

His expression intent, Andrei said, "We don't actually do the blood ceremony anymore. It's merely an expression."

Pretty certain he was placating her, she figured dropping the subject was in her best interests. "Oh, all right, then."

She tried to pull away, but Andrei hung on to her hand and drew her closer.

"Instead of the blood, we can use a kiss to seal the bargain."

Her bones threatened to melt at the suggestion, and she realized that part of her—the young, silly part that hadn't quite grown up—*wanted* him to kiss her. His eyes had narrowed to slits and his nostrils flared as he stared at her from beneath long, thick lashes. He drew so close, she could feel his breath on her face, and yet he hesitated. How ridiculous—he was merely baiting her for his own amusement.

"One more thing, Lizzie."

Elizabeth licked her lips in preparation to protest. But all she could eek out was "What?"

"The killer is still out there. Be very careful. I don't want you to end up like your mother."

She started. "My mother? You mean...dead?" A terrible thrill shot through her as she protested, "But I have no enemies."

"Alas, Lizzie, by aligning yourself with me on this, you do."

Without warning, he tugged her against him and claimed her lips in a hard, fast kiss that nevertheless sent her reeling. Thrown back ten years, she remembered another such kiss—and the frantic lovemaking that had followed.

But not now. This time he released her and she had to catch herself from falling.

"Tonight," he said, "after the carnival closes we'll compare notes."

Then she stood there, senses on hold, as Andrei stalked away from her and onto the midway, where he was swallowed by the crowd.

"Oh," she murmured, fingers touching lips that tingled and demanded more.

Well, there wouldn't be more. She would make certain of that. The carnival would be gone in a few days, and until then she needed a clear head to deal with Andrei Sobatka. A clear head to learn the truth.

The truth...could they really find it after ten years? They had to, or possibly an innocent man would die and a guilty one would go free.

Her mind whirled with the responsibility she was taking on.

If neither Carlo nor her father had killed her mother—and she was certain her father hadn't—then who had?

Chapter Three

On her way out of the house that afternoon to carry through with her end of the bargain, Elizabeth hesitated when the telephone rang.

She could let the answering machine pick up...but she didn't.

"Elizabeth," came her father's stern voice from the other end. "I've heard a disturbing rumor."

"Daddy." Her mouth went dry, but she forced out the words. "Rumor? Which would be?"

"That you're seeing that Andrei Sobatka again. I thought we settled that."

"There's nothing romantic about my seeing him, Daddy," she said, hedging.

"Then what's going on?"

Elizabeth hated this. Her father was still in Baton Rouge and would be there until the following afternoon. She'd hoped to have some answers before she'd had to tell him anything.

"It's about Mama," she said. "Rather, Mama's killer."

"Mustov's appeals are up, sweetheart. Nothing to worry about there. The execution will go on as scheduled next week."

"That's the problem. I'm not sure he did it."

"Of course he did it!"

Elizabeth didn't answer immediately. She couldn't not ask him...yet how could she?

"Daddy," she began breathlessly, trying to phrase her question carefully, "why didn't you ever tell anyone that you knew that Mama was having an affair with Carlo Mustov?"

"How can you ask me such a thing?"

He sounded indignant, but she noted he didn't deny it.

"Because I saw a copy of a letter that Mama wrote to him. She said you knew about Carlo and that you were very angry about it. I remember the two of you fighting, Daddy. I tried shutting myself off from it, because you'd been fighting so much, but I know that you were angry with her."

"Not angry enough to kill her," he said, a chill in his stiff tone.

I hope not.

She thought the words, but she didn't voice them. She didn't know what to say, in fact. Her father was being evasive about this even now.

"That damn Sobatka's got you all worked up for nothing, sweetheart," he said, his voice suddenly so silky it shot a warning note up her spine. "Promise me you'll let it alone, that you won't see him again."

"I can't do that, Daddy. I need to make sure you're not implicated in Mama's death."

That was true. She only prayed he believed her.

ANDREI KNEW he'd been right to warn Lizzie—it assuaged his unease about involving her. Not that he had any reason to feel guilty. She had come to him, after all. Remembering how stubborn she could be, he knew she was determined to prove her father innocent, no matter the danger to herself.

That was the way with *gadje,* he thought. They would never believe one of their own was guilty. Better to blame a Rom.

As someone caught between both worlds, he could see both sides of the equation. And if the carnival wasn't here in Les Baux, he would investigate both sides, as well, and keep Lizzie out of this. But the people here in this town knew only one side of him. To them, to Lizzie, he was Romany, Gypsy, no matter that his mother was *gadji* and had sent him to his Creole grandmother in New Orleans to be tamed and educated every winter after he'd reached puberty. None of that was known to the townspeople here. None of that mattered. Not to them.

Not to Miss Elizabeth Granville, who still saw him as the Gypsy boy she'd once had under her spell.

She might have him again, Andrei thought ruefully as a familiar itch grew. Thinking about Lizzie did that to him—tortured him, because there was nothing he could do to relieve himself.

Damn Valonia! he thought, then instantly regretted cursing the dead woman. She'd had valid reason to want revenge for what had happened to her son.

But he hadn't been involved, so why had she cursed him? He couldn't think of anything worse than wanting a woman only to fail at the crucial moment.

Andrei set out to keep his end of the bargain, while wondering how well Lizzie would keep hers. It was to her advantage to conclude that Carlo was indeed the murderer, though to be fair, he didn't think she would want an innocent man to die for her mother's death. And surely she would want the guilty one punished.

As long as it wasn't her father of course.

Twice now, he'd sensed some kind of guilt in her, but for once, he hadn't been able to interpret the confusing emotion. No doubt it had to do with the senator and her defense of him—she didn't know who else had a motive for the murder any more than he did.

Making the rounds of the carnival, he questioned a few of the old-timers—Gregor, who ran the Ferris wheel and acted as consulting mechanic on all the rides, and Dorina, in charge of food and whose recipe for funnel cake had been in use ever since he was a boy. Both had been good friends with Valonia and Carlo. Neither had anything to say about Carlo's *gadji,* however, except that it was a shame one so young had to lose her life.

Next, Andrei set out to find Tony, who'd been good friends with Carlo—the men had hung out together. But before he got far, Andrei heard the tinkling of bracelets and turned around to find Florica following him. When she realized he'd spotted her, she smiled and tossed her hair back from her shoulders.

"How is the prettiest Rom at the carnival today?" Andrei asked.

Florica giggled as she danced around him. "Do you like my hair? The old style made me look too young."

Andrei stared. Her hair was long and loose, the same as always. "So you've changed it," he said, not letting doubt creep into his tone.

"So much more grown-up than braids, don't you think?"

Braids? She hadn't worn braids for years and years, not since she was a little girl. But all he said was "Lovely."

He knew Florica's mind fluttered back and forth through time, which could be a fortunate thing for him, considering his mission had to do with the past.

"Real men like messy hair," Florica said, raising her eyebrows and twirling for him.

That was what he'd told the customer to get her on the Tilt-a-Whirl earlier. Andrei didn't remember seeing Florica around at the time, but Lizzie had distracted him. Besides, Florica often flitted here and there like a will-o'-the-wisp. She must have overheard him, and no doubt she would use that line for years to come. Though the woman was childlike, she had a better grasp of what was going on than most believed. And when she concentrated, her memory went deep.

"Florica, I need to talk to you. Do you have a few minutes?"

"Papa did want me to come right back." She seemed torn, her features drawing into a scowl. "He'll be very angry with me again." Then they softened. "But for you, Andrei…"

"Let's sit."

He led her toward a picnic table under the trees and away from the food trailers. Because it was early, the area was nearly empty but for a couple and a family of six. While Andrei sat on a bench, Florica stayed in motion. A fallen log lay to one side of the picnic area, and she seemed fascinated with circling it. She took precise little steps, all the while holding her long skirts up several inches from her sandaled feet.

"Florica, you remember Carlo, don't you?"

"Carlo?" She continued circling. "I'm mad at him. He was supposed to take me to a movie last week, but he forgot."

"He didn't forget," Andrei said gently, realizing her *last week* had come and gone ten years before. "He's in jail, remember? For killing Theresa Granville."

Florica stopped and frowned. "The *gadji*. Everyone said she was no good for him."

Picking up on that immediately, Andrei asked, "Who is everyone?"

But the young woman had slipped into her own world. She was on the log now, doing a balancing act as she traversed its rough length.

"Florica, did you ever hear anyone speak harshly about Theresa Granville?"

"Papa didn't like her. He said she would bring about ruin and destruction." Her voice was small and childlike. "She was a wicked, wicked woman. Married with a daughter and whoring with Carlo. She *did* ruin Carlo just like Papa said. He's in jail now," she finished as if Andrei hadn't just reminded her.

"And if we don't help him, Carlo will die."

"Carlo's dead, Carlo's dead," she singsonged to herself. "He's out of my heart and out of my head."

"He's not dead *yet!*" Andrei declared. "We still have a chance to save him. If only we can find the real killer…"

Florica stared at him through the curtain of hair that had fallen across her face. Her mouth was open, her lips moving, but no words were issued.

"Can you help me, Florica?" Andrei said. "Carlo was your friend, wasn't he? Just like I'm your friend?"

She nodded and for a moment he caught a glimpse of lucidity crossing her narrow features. "Carlo's being convicted of the *gadji*'s murder broke my heart."

"Then help me—"

"And my heart will be broken again," she said, her gaze boring into him.

"Why do you say that?"

"Bad things happen here in Les Baux," she whispered. "Bad things could happen to you, too."

A chill shot down Andrei's spine. He pushed himself up from the bench. Did she know something or not?

Gently taking her hand, he asked, "What bad things?"

But Florica was already gone, withdrawn into her secret world, a world that even he with his magic could not enter. Rom magic had never worked on Florica, undoubtedly because mentally she was…different. Andrei shook off his disappointment. He would get no more from her today.

"Florica, I think you'd better go home, or Milo will worry."

"Papa?" she said, her focus turning outward again, but away from Andrei. She pulled her hand free and stepped down off the log. "I'm coming, Papa," she singsonged, then hurried toward the trailers as if she'd actually heard him calling.

Leaving Andrei staring after her, knowing no more than he had earlier, and wondering why he'd ever thought he could succeed where his cousins had failed.

THE END OF THE DAY brought no cheer to Elizabeth, who'd been in more Les Baux front parlors than she'd visited in years. She was hot and sweaty and more than anything wanted to jump in the bayou for a swim on the way to her late-night meeting with Andrei at the carnival.

The swim being a fantasy of course. The bayou was for alligators; the shower or tub for Granvilles.

So it had always been, so it would always be, she thought, undoing the top few buttons of her blouse and unsticking it from where it clung to her skin. *Better.* Next she removed her jacket and stifled the rash impulse to take off her shoes and panty hose, as well. She really should shower and change, she thought, but the notion still clung that her conservative clothing could serve as armor to protect her from Andrei Sobatka.

Despite her knowing that no matter what she wore, what she said, he could read her like a book. Always had. He was a man who knew women. At least he knew her.

Too bad she hadn't known *him* as well as she'd thought.

She'd barely entered the carnival grounds when she heard a voice come out of the night. "Looking for someone, Lizzie?"

Elizabeth whipped around to face her nemesis, who was leaning against a tree to one side of the office trailer. Though the moon was nearly full, a cloud hid most of it, so she could barely see him there. But she had the impression of lean strength and something powerful, dark, coiled and ready to explode.

"Andrei, you startled me," she gasped.

"Feeling guilty about something?"

"What? No."

"Then why are you so nervous?" He pushed away from the shadows.

As if he didn't know.

Andrei drew closer, crowding her, but Elizabeth refused to give ground. Her mistake. Heat rekindled and sparked and oozed through her pores. Her breasts ached and her center burned for his touch.

Dear Lord, she wanted him. Right here. Right now.

Of course she couldn't act on this desire. She wouldn't act on it!

She wished for a moment that she wasn't such a "lady." But that was just a fancy that rankled deep within her.

"So what new information do you have about my mother's death?" she snapped.

"Unfortunately, nothing."

"Just as I expected." She sensed him bristle at what surely sounded like a criticism.

"What? You think I didn't try?" He crowded her back against the tree. "I spent every minute of my free time talking to people who were with the carnival the summer your mother was murdered."

"I didn't mean that you didn't try—I know how desperately you want information that would free Carlo. It just seems that the information is nonexistent."

But explanations didn't take the edge off the tension wiring between them, attracting and repelling simultaneously. If only he wasn't standing so close. If only he wasn't so interested in her blouse where she'd unbuttoned it. Andrei's gaze seemed to be riveted by what he saw there. Elizabeth wanted to do the buttons back up, but she refused to give him the satisfaction of knowing he'd unnerved her. Instead, she tried to remain casual, to pretend that he had no effect on her whatsoever.

"I didn't learn anything new, either," she said in a miraculously even voice.

"No juicy tidbits from Miss Ina?"

He leaned in and reached out, not to touch her, but to place a hand on the tree trunk mere inches from her head.

"I...I didn't see her, after all." She could hardly concentrate. Could hardly get a cohesive sentence together. "Miss Ina's daughter brought her to New Orleans for a few days' visit. She should be back tomorrow. But if you want to know the truth," she said breathlessly, "I think we're on a wild-goose chase."

"You mean, you still think Carlo did it and you're resenting the hell out of me for putting you through some minor discomfort.''

''Don't put words in my mouth. I hate that.''

''You have enough experience. As I remember, you were always mouthing your daddy's opinions.''

''That was ten years ago!''

''What's changed?'' Andrei asked. ''You still work for him and live with him and defend him.''

''He doesn't have anyone else.''

Nor did she. And no one else had ever suggested that she couldn't be her own person just because she remained close with her surviving parent.

Looking for a way to throw him off, Elizabeth asked, ''And what does your coming back to the carnival say about you? You don't belong here anymore. You should have a real life with a home and a woman who's crazy about you—''

''Not in this lifetime,'' he growled.

''Why?'' she asked, wondering what had happened to sour him on relationships. ''Because you can't commit yourself to anyone?''

''You don't know anything about me.''

She laughed and said, ''I know enough,'' and tried to push by him.

But he wouldn't budge, and when she tried to duck around him, he shot his free arm out to the tree, so that one hand lay against the bark on either side of her face. She was surrounded by him.

''Andrei, let me go.''

Her eyes had adjusted to the dark now, and she easily saw the smile tugging at his mouth.

''So you can go back to that big house with no one waiting for you?''

''Daddy—''

"—is in Baton Rouge."

A breeze picked up and fanned her overheated body. "What do you care?" she asked softly. "What is it you want from me, Andrei?"

"This."

His head swooped down as fast as that of a bird of prey, and he had her, then, mouth to mouth, chest to breast, hips to hips, her back pressed into the tree trunk. Reminded of her first sexual encounter—a moment in time spent with *him*—her body came alive.

His assault was aggressive and tender and coaxing. His tongue gentle and bold and clever. His teeth sharp and quick and teasing.

No one on earth could kiss like Andrei Sobatka, Elizabeth thought, surrendering to the magic, fearing that if he moved back now, she would puddle at his feet.

This wasn't a learned skill, but one he'd been born with. She'd known that from the first time he'd kissed her—and he'd barely been legal then. Over the years, she'd tried to find someone who could outdo him in the kissing department. Maybe then she could have forgotten him.

But she'd never found his match in any man when it came to kissing—or anything else.

By the time Andrei came up for air, Elizabeth was panting, ready and willing to take the next step.

But his step was back and away from her, his arms falling to his sides. She leaned back into the tree to keep from falling at his feet.

"Run, Lizzie," he said softly. "Run away home before we both have reason to regret your hesitating."

Something about the way he said that disturbed her. He sounded torn...no, tortured.

"What is it?" She wanted to move to him, so that she

could read him better, but she didn't dare leave the support of the tree trunk. "What's troubling you?"

"You are. We don't belong together, Lizzie, so there's no fooling ourselves, now is there."

Her fingers bit into the bark. He thought she was fooling herself?

Desire evaporated like sweat in a desert. One second it was there, the next it was gone.

Angry and frustrated, thinking he still didn't know his own mind regarding her after all these years, Elizabeth took his advice for perhaps the first time and headed right past him and straight for home.

THE GRANVILLE WOMAN fled the scene, and her would-be lover followed part of the way before veering off in the direction of the trailers.

Two more problems to take care of—was there no end to them?

The wind picked up and whistled eerily through the trees. You would think a wind like that would blow off some of the humidity, but not deep in bayou country. Rather, it stirred the swamp stink and cast it over the nearby land, turning the air fetid, like the smell of death.

On just such a night ten years before, Theresa Granville had drawn her last breath.

She haunted this place, haunted those involved.

It should have been over long ago—Carlo Mustov would be dead now, but for the appeals process. Then no one would be prying and poking and stirring up things best left alone. Do-gooders—their numbers kept increasing, if not their sense of self-preservation.

If Andrei Sobatka and Elizabeth Granville thought they'd been discreet discussing their bargain to find her mother's real killer here on carnival grounds, they'd been sadly mistaken.

Whatever information they hoped to find, they were bound to be disappointed.

No one knew anything that would clear Carlo.

At least no one who would tell.

Why couldn't they all just back off? Why start digging now, after all these years? Why make themselves targets—and for what?

Carlo Mustov *was* going to die and soon.

The question was, how many would have to join him?

Chapter Four

"Elizabeth, dear, it's such a pleasure to have you for a visit. It's been far too long. Since the last election, if I remember correctly."

Miss Ina remembered *exactly,* Elizabeth thought with satisfaction, counting on that memory going back even further. They sat in the elderly woman's front parlor, a tea service laid out on the spindly-legged table. Elizabeth had wedged herself in one corner of the ancient couch with its faded flowered upholstery, while Miss Ina sat in a rose-colored wing-backed chair and poured tea.

Taking the porcelain cup from the frail hand heavy with rings, Elizabeth said, "I have to admit to an ulterior motive in coming to see you today, Miss Ina."

The silver-haired octogenarian looked at her through eyes that were still sharp behind frameless glasses. "What office does your daddy intend to run for this time?"

"It's not about Daddy. It's Mama."

"Theresa? But she's been dead for…let me think a moment…about ten years, I believe."

Elizabeth nodded. "And Carlo Mustov is still on death row for her murder."

"Then what is the problem?"

"I'm no longer convinced that he's guilty."

"Oh, my."

"But I can't figure out who else might have killed Mama, either."

Miss Ina stared down into her teacup. "I don't know how I can I help you."

"You knew Mama pretty well."

"Yes, she was such a dear girl. She used to make a point of coming to see me when I couldn't get out."

"The two of you talked, then."

"Of course."

"About her? Her problems, I mean."

Miss Ina frowned. "Theresa wasn't much on volunteering that kind of information."

"Oh." Disappointment flooded Elizabeth, making her wonder why she was on this fool's mission.

"But then, I've always had a way of getting things out of people when they were troubled," the old woman admitted. "What exactly might you want to know?"

"Whether anyone had reason to hate Mama…enough to kill her."

"Oh, my, no! Everyone loved her."

Elizabeth remembered saying the very same thing to Andrei. And she in turn echoed him. "Not everyone."

"Well, I don't think her being too pretty or too well dressed or too involved with the community was her downfall."

"You think it was Carlo, then."

"I'm not sure." Miss Ina put down her cup. "She told me she was having an affair with Carlo. I wasn't shocked, you understand. I'm old. I've seen and heard it all. I was merely concerned for her. And for you. I felt she needed some perspective on her situation, so I told her to break it off with him, because he wasn't worth losing everything over. She agreed. That was the day before she died. Too bad I didn't speak up sooner. Then, I had no idea that 'everything' included her life.''

"When you spoke to her so frankly, did Mama say anything about being afraid of Carlo?"

"No. But she admitted to being uncomfortable in her situation with him. She said she felt someone was watching them. It gave her...I believe she said it gave her the creeps. Yes. And that she feared the person would either blackmail her or go to your daddy and tell him everything.''

Wondering if her mother had been right, Elizabeth closed her eyes for a moment, then said, "Well, thank you, Miss Ina. I appreciate your being so frank with me.''

If only the information hadn't pointed potential guilt back to her father.

JUSTICE IS BLIND. *Love is death. The law is impotent.*

And he was living proof, Andrei thought as he spoke to his mother long distance on the phone in the trailer office.

"I wish I could tell you that I've remembered something in addition to what I testified," his mother said, "but I can't. Believe me, I've gone over their argument in my head more times than I can count. I so hate that Carlo was convicted on my testimony.''

"Do you believe he could be innocent, Maman?"

"I simply don't know. 'You can't think I'll simply step aside. You'll never be free of me, Theresa.' That is what he said. His exact words. They haunt me still.''

He was getting nowhere fast, Andrei thought. All he'd managed to do was get himself involved with the one woman he should have avoided. The one woman who'd had it in her power to tempt him into making a fool of himself.

As if his mother knew what he was thinking, she asked "Andrei, how are you?"

"The same."

"You don't sound the same. I hear tension in your voice."

"Well, trying to clear Carlo is every bit as stressful as I thought it would be."

"No, it's something else."

"No. There's nothing."

He heard her sigh before she said, "I am your mother Any time you want to talk, you know I'm here for you.'

"I know that and I love you for it."

But his mother was the last person in the world he could talk to about this particular problem. And he certainly wouldn't discuss it here, where anyone could walk in and overhear. Not liking the whole idea of cell phones he refused to buy one for himself. So he wound up the conversation and rang off before his mother could probe more deeply or someone walked in.

But he couldn't forget about it. Couldn't forget Valonia's curse that would undoubtedly shadow him for the rest of his natural life.

Mood dark, he left the office and headed for the midway.

"Andrei, there you are!"

Recognizing Alessandra's voice, he turned as his cousin caught up to him.

He hugged her and gave her a worried look. "You shouldn't be here, not by yourself. Where's Wyatt?"

"At home, where he needs to be. He's better, though And itching to finish what he started before the carniva picks up and moves to the next town. He's hoping the doctor will clear him for less restricted activity at his follow-up appointment tomorrow."

Andrei moved off toward his trailer, Alessandra at his side. He said, "Don't let him rush into anything he shouldn't."

"I don't want him to. On the other hand, he's an experienced investigator and we don't have much time. Rather, Carlo doesn't. Barely a week before the execution."

A truly grim reality, Andrei thought. "Sabina and Garner and Elizabeth and I are all on it."

Arriving at his trailer, she put a hand on his arm and stopped him from going in. "Elizabeth?"

"Elizabeth Granville."

Alessandra's eyes went wide. "You mean the victim's daughter?"

"The same."

"But why would she want to help us?"

"Because she doesn't want the wrong man to die. Because she wants justice for her mother's sake. Because I convinced her that your aunt's murder and the attacks on all of you gave her reasonable doubt."

In deference to Alessandra's respect for Rom tradition, he didn't speak the dead woman's name.

"Hmm, why do I get the feeling there's more going on here than her being reasonable?"

"Nothing is going on." Only in his own mind.

Alessandra took his hand and studied it for a moment. It was a superstition that Rom fortune-tellers never read the palms of their own. But Alessandra had a true gift.

And so when she said, "But not because you don't want more…. Andrei, this Elizabeth, she wouldn't be the Lizzie you used to moon over when we were young, would she?" Andrei got nervous and pulled his hand away.

He shook his head. "She's not Lizzie anymore."

"Aha." She gave him a knowing look. "Semantics, Andrei. So what *isn't* going on?"

"Did anyone ever tell you that you can be annoying, little cousin?"

Alessandra gave him a sad smile. "So a woman finally has your heart and she doesn't want it? In a way, that serves you right for all those women you loved and left."

Thinking of the women who couldn't fill the void left by Lizzie, Andrei said, "You don't know anything about it."

"I'm not an innocent. I know about your women."

"Past tense," he insisted. "Very past."

Her expression disbelieving, she said, "Oh, please—"

"Wyatt and Garner weren't the only ones cursed, remember."

He didn't know what made him bring that up. They hadn't discussed it. He'd never before admitted his problem to anyone but Sabina, who'd explained the curse.

A number of emotions crossed her features. And then, quietly, Alessandra said, "*The law is impotent.* Oh, Andrei, I just hadn't thought about it, I guess."

"No pity, please."

"Not pity. Sorrow, perhaps. For how long?"

"Long enough that I've felt cursed." He barked a laugh. "Which, indeed, I was!"

"Surely it's reversible."

"Right, go ask your aunt how to do that. Oh, no, you can't. She's dead and has taken her secrets to the grave."

"But Wyatt got his sight back and my aunt did nothing to help him," Alessandra said. "And Garner didn't lose Sabina. Somehow, something intervened.... Maybe true love."

"Well, that doesn't give me much hope."

"Don't sell yourself short. You've always done that, ever since we were kids."

"I was just realistic about being Gypsy in a *gadje* world."

She shook her head. "You were always so defiant. It was as if you wanted to point to yourself and say, 'Look at me, because I'm different than you.'"

"I was. I am. We both are."

"All children feel that way. Most teenagers, too. But you always wanted to fight about it. Andrei, haven't you learned that when people get to know you, they forget what you're supposed to be and see who you really are? Maybe Elizabeth—your Lizzie—will do the same."

For the longest time, Andrei had hoped so.

Year after year, the carnival had stopped at Les Baux, and Andrei had watched Lizzie grow from a snooty little girl into a society belle with a cool, aloof facade. Even so, he'd recognized the fire that burned deep inside her, for it burned in him, as well.

That she'd been no easy town girl had earned his grudging respect. The night of her debutante ball, he had watched hungrily from the hotel veranda as she'd completed her dance card with awkward teenage boys of her own social class.

He'd never felt more of an outsider, and yet, for a brief shining moment, he'd dared to hope that he could be more.

With her.

Andrei couldn't tell Alessandra all that. Recognizing they were entering dangerous waters, he decided to turn the conversation back around to her.

"You never did tell me what you're doing here."

"Looking for you." Her eyes suddenly filled with tears. "I'm told the medical examiner will probably release my aunt's body in the next day or two, so I'm going to start making arrangements for the burial. I know this is a lot to ask, but...will you be a pallbearer?''

"Of course." Not for the woman who had cursed him, but for Alessandra and Sabina.

"Thank you, Andrei. You haven't seen Tony, have you?''

Figuring she wanted to ask Carlo's best friend, as well, he shook his head. "No one has seen him for over a week—he seems to have taken off.''

Alessandra frowned. "I don't understand. He's been with the carnival ever since I can remember. He wouldn't just leave without telling someone.''

"Unless he had good reason.''

"As in?''

"A lot of bad things have happened in the short time we've been here...''

"You think Tony's involved?''

"I don't like to think so, but why else would he have disappeared?'' He shrugged, then asked, "What about the contents of your aunt's trailer and tent?''

"Anything that isn't considered evidence is released as of now.''

They both fell silent for a moment, and Andrei figured they were thinking along the same lines. Valonia's private possessions would be burned or destroyed in Romany tradition.

"When?'' he asked.

"Tonight. Midnight.''

As MIDNIGHT APPROACHED, the rides were shut down, the tents closed, and tension filled the air.

Word had gotten round, and the carnies were steeling themselves for what was about to happen. Some of the men were stacking wood for a bonfire in the parking lot. The area had been cleared of brush, so that it would be unlikely the fire could spread if the wind picked up. Under Alessandra's directions, the women were going through Valonia's things and carrying them to the area where the ritual would be performed.

Andrei planned to join Alessandra shortly. Wyatt couldn't be there, and Sabina and Garner were still in Baton Rouge, and this observance couldn't wait. Valonia's possessions should have been destroyed immediately after her death, and if not for the police investigation, they would have been.

But at the moment Andrei was preoccupied with wondering where the devil Lizzie was and trying to fix the blasted Tilt-a-Whirl before he had to pack it up the next day and move on to the next town.

All night, the ride had limped along with few thrills for anyone. The mechanism was old of course, and though Andrei was an engineer in his real life—or had been until he'd quit his job to rejoin the carnival and his clan—he was having a hell of a time figuring out what was wrong in his life, whether it was a woman or a piece of faulty equipment. Thinking about the imminent move, he knew he didn't have much time to fix things with Lizzie, either. Or to find a murderer.

Andrei stepped into one of the cars and leaned against the cushioned seat.

As he bent over the outside of the car to run his flashlight beam around the equipment, a low keening in the distance raised the short hairs at the back of his neck. Mourners were beginning to express their grief, and he couldn't do anything but listen and close his eyes in a brief prayer for the woman who had cursed him.

The moment's inattention served him poorly, for when the ride suddenly and mysteriously started with a jerk, Andrei dropped the flashlight, lost his balance and took a nosedive straight over the side.

Chapter Five

The late-night activity and low keen of voices put an edge on the night and a pebble to her skin as Elizabeth searched through the crowd in vain for Andrei. She should have been here some time ago, but after talking to Miss Ina, she'd tried to reach her father in Baton Rouge to ask him how he found out about Mama and Carlo.

He wasn't home, wasn't, apparently, even in the capital city.

It was as if he had vanished.

Coming in sight of the moving Tilt-a-Whirl, she straightened the skirt of her sundress and called out to him.

Andrei's name turned into a gasp lost in the sound of the ride when she spotted him hanging half-off one of the cars and by sheer will, it seemed, clinging to the metal bars with both hands and one leg as the car whipped around faster and faster.

As Andrei fought the centrifugal force, Elizabeth ran toward him, looking around wildly for help. She thought she saw a shadow move behind the ride, but she blinked and the shadow was gone.

Somehow Andrei pulled himself back into the car and managed to right himself, but he was still off balance as the Tilt-a-Whirl careered faster than she'd ever seen it work.

"Andrei, how do I stop it?" she yelled, but she doubted he heard her over the screech of machinery.

Despite the movement of the car, Andrei stared steadily at the operator's panel to the side of the ride. Elizabeth's gaze followed his and she saw the levers. That was it! But before she could get to them, one of them began to tremble and then move by itself!

Nearly tripping over her own feet, Elizabeth flashed a wide-eyed look at Andrei—who seemed to be concentrating hard—then back to the magically lifting metal rod. Immediately she was reminded of the other day when he'd given those teenage girls such a thrill ride.

Could Andrei somehow be making the lever move without touching it?

Suddenly the lever flipped up flat against the board, and the Tilt-a-Whirl shuddered to a dead stop. Andrei jumped to the ground and she flew into his arms.

"My Lord, I thought you were going to be hurt!" she cried, throwing her arms around him and wildly covering his face with kisses. "Thank God you're all right!"

And then she couldn't talk at all because Andrei was kissing her in return. This wasn't a sweet, seductive kiss but one filled with desperation and long-denied feelings. Before she knew it, Elizabeth was lost in emotion.

Reminded of a similar kiss from her youth, she reveled in the memory...

Uninspired by the boys she danced with at her debutante ball, put off by the fight between her parents, which ruined the evening for her, she imagined being in Andrei's arms on the dance floor as she walked home alone along the bayou.

Then suddenly he was there.

Beneath a full moon, the most exciting boy she'd ever met had spun her in his arms across the dew-laden ground to music only they could hear. Thoroughly beguiled by him, she gave him hot kisses. Her virginity. Her love.

But in the morning, her mother was found dead, and the alleged murderer was another Gypsy, a friend of Andrei's.

And Elizabeth realized that while she'd lain with a man for the first time, her mother had lain alone, dying...

That part of the memory shattered the emotions building in her now, and she immediately ended the kiss and whirled back into the present, with its eery wail of human sound. She was shaking and her body was alive in a way that it had only been once before.

"Lizzie?"

Appalled to realize that she was in love with Andrei still, Elizabeth drew back and shut him out the best she could. Huddled with her arms wrapped around her middle, shaken to her very core, she stared at him, guilt eating at her now as it had that horrific morning.

The full moon silvered Andrei's features, making him suddenly seem distant.

And relieved.

When she could find her voice, she asked, "What happened? With the ride," she was quick to clarify.

She wanted nothing personal between them...

...she wanted everything personal between them.

"The Tilt-a-Whirl wasn't working properly and I was trying to fix it. Then the ride just started by itself."

"No, not by itself. Someone was there," she said, pointing to the area where she'd seen the shadow.

Andrei jogged behind the ride, and she followed more slowly. She needed time to regain a calm demeanor. To regain her poise.

"Whoever did this to you certainly knows how this equipment works," she mused as she caught up to him. "That wouldn't be Daddy."

Looking around as if he could find who'd stood here just moments ago, he nodded. "You have a point. And the other ride jockeys were kids when your mother was murdered—except for Gregor, who's a gentle old man—so we can exclude them, as well."

Which left whom?

"How did you stop the ride?" she asked. "How did you move that lever?"

"Must have been the vibration," he said.

"Liar!"

He didn't deny it.

When he crouched low over the ground, she asked, "What are you looking for?" She knew pressing him for a truth he didn't want to share would do her no good.

"I'm checking out the footprints."

"It all looks like a muddle to me."

"That's because more than one person has been back here." Suddenly he reached for something and retrieved it.

"What is it?"

"A coin." Rising, he showed her a coin unlike anything she'd ever seen.

"Not U.S. currency."

"It belongs to Milo Vasilli," Andrei said grimly. "He flips it when he's nervous."

"He would know how to work the ride, wouldn't he?" she asked.

"That he would." Andrei seemed thoughtful as he dropped the coin into his pocket. "What puzzles me is what he might have had against your mother."

"Then you think he's the—?"

He shrugged. "He would have no reason."

They stared at each other for a moment, and Elizabeth wanted in the worst way to close the gap again, to be held in comforting arms for one sweet moment more. But suddenly Andrei turned, took her hand and pulled her along with him.

"Where are we going?"

"To the parking lot."

The keening voices...

The lament grew louder as they drew nearer. In the middle of the open area, a hot orange ball danced and flickered, dark silhouettes surrounding it, swaying to some mournful beat. A bonfire.

Elizabeth saw one woman take an armful of what looked like bedding and throw it into the flames. And then another tossed in what surely were garments. A third shawls and shoes.

And then a crash, like that of glass, made Elizabeth stop in her tracks and raised the skin along her spine.

"What's going on?" she asked.

"Valonia's possessions are being burned or destroyed."

"Why?"

"*Marime.* Contamination. Rom avoid touching their dead and get rid of their possessions."

"Everything?"

"All but what will go into the ground with Valonia— her best clothing, her jewelry, her favorite shawl. Photographs of Carlo and Alessandra and Sabina will also be placed in the coffin with her to accompany her on her spiritual journey to the next world," Andrei explained. "In some clans, even her trailer would be burned. But because the carnival is just squeaking by, Valonia's trailer will be sold to some *gadjo* and the money will be put in a fund to be used where needed. Another Rom would never take the possessions of the dead,'' he concluded. ''And the clan will avoid speaking her name.''

''But *you* have been using it.''

''Yes.'' He didn't explain.

Elizabeth asked, ''What are they afraid of?''

''That she'll return in some supernatural form to haunt them. The thing they fear most is her *mulo* escaping from the body and seeking revenge on anyone who might have harmed her.''

''Like her murderer?'' Elizabeth whispered, thinking of her own mother.

As if he could read her mind, Andrei squeezed her hand. They stood there, silent, paying their respects to the dead woman as the clan forever obliterated Valonia's life on earth.

ANDREI GAZED around the bonfire but didn't see Milo. Though a rage was building in him, he was keeping it under control. Rages were to be avoided. Ever since he'd become impotent, his power to move objects with his mind had become stronger, as if all his energies were being unnaturally channeled into that one area. In the grip of rage, he might not be able to control his telekinesis.

So Milo wasn't paying his respects to Valonia. And it appeared he was keeping Florica from doing so, as well. No doubt they were in their trailer.

When the frenzy around the bonfire died down and the clan stood there, heads bowed in prayer, Andrei tugged Elizabeth's hand and led her away.

She waited until they were halfway to the trailers before asking, ''Where now?''

''To find Milo Vasilli. Curious that a leader is nowhere to be seen, almost as if he had reason *not* to be here.''

"What reason?" Elizabeth asked, but Andrei simply kept going without saying another word.

Not that he had to. Elizabeth got it.

First they'd found Milo's coin behind the ride, and now it seemed he wasn't mourning Valonia's death. Because he feared her *mulo?*

If so, that would mean...

Heart pounding, Elizabeth took a deep breath and kept step with Andrei as they entered the trailer area.

Was it about to happen at last? Would she come face-to-face with the man who murdered her mother?

Suddenly she heard a sharp crash from inside one of the trailers. Andrei pulled her into the shadows beneath the window of the trailer.

Through the window drifted a familiar, childlike voice. "You've been very, very bad, Papa. Very, very sinful."

"I only did what was necessary to protect you, as always!" a man shouted in return.

Then the trailer door burst open and Milo stalked off into the dark. Still holding Elizabeth's hand, Andrei started after him. The tinkling sound of jewelry turned them both toward the trailer doorway as the young woman who'd told Elizabeth about the Tilt-a-Whirl stepped outside.

"Andrei!" she cried, her smile brilliant.

Andrei hesitated. "Florica, do you know where your father went off to?"

Florica's smile died suddenly, and Elizabeth realized the young woman was staring down at her and Andrei's tightly entwined hands.

A look of confusion crossed her features, then she giggled and said, "Bad things happen in Les Baux. If you're not careful, Andrei, something bad could happen to you."

"Bad how?" Andrei asked, but Florica had taken a

sudden great interest in her hair. She was winding a strand round and round her fingers.

"Don't you like my new hairstyle, Andrei?"

"Florica, who would do this bad thing?" he asked. "Your papa?"

She began chanting, "Papa's mad...Papa's bad... Papa's mad...Papa's bad..."

Andrei shook his head. "Come on, Lizzie, we're not going to get anything more out of her."

As he led her off, Elizabeth glanced back over her shoulder. Florica was turning in a circle, seemingly listening to inner voices. Her heart went out to the woman. What had happened, she wondered, to the poor girl's mind?

Though the moon was full, it scudded behind a bank of clouds as they cut through the small trailer park and came out in a rough, overgrown area.

"Do you really think we'll find Milo?" she asked.

"Why not? He doesn't know we're on his trail."

Trail? What trail? The man had disappeared into the night. But Andrei kept going as though he could see in the dark. Indeed, his movements were sleek and catlike, while she was merely clumsy. She tripped once and would have fallen onto her knees if he hadn't caught her.

The moon peeked out from the clouds, and she got a good look at their surroundings.

"I know this place," she murmured, suddenly chilled even though the night was summer hot and humid. "This is where my mother's body was found."

The ancient live oak was straight ahead. And through the dripping moss, she saw movement near the thick trunk.

"Milo," Andrei growled softly, pulling her from the clearing and into the trees.

Swiftly, they moved forward and Elizabeth heard a low, deep drone—Milo muttering to himself. Perhaps Florica was not the only one in the family who'd lost her mind.

Milo's back was to them. They crept closer as the carnival owner reached into a hollow in the trunk of the live oak.

"What is that?" she whispered as Milo withdrew a packet wrapped in cloth.

Andrei put a finger to his lips and indicated she should stay put while he moved forward.

She watched Milo as he unfolded the cloth from around some hard object. Caught for a moment, she didn't move. The cloth fell to the ground and the object in his hand glinted under the moonlight.

Her eyes widened as he held up a knife and began keening as loudly as the mourners had earlier.

"Mama!" she whispered, certain that what he held was the weapon that had been missing all these years—the knife that had been used to kill her mother!

Chapter Six

Andrei drew close enough to Milo to see the moongleam off the knife's sharp edge and the fancy carving on the handle. "So, that's the murder weapon?"

"What?" Milo's head jerked up, and he looked around wildly. "Andrei!"

Shock altered his voice and twisted his features into someone Andrei didn't recognize.

"Yes, Milo," he said. "I'm still alive and uninjured, no thanks to you. But Theresa Granville wasn't so lucky. Is that the knife you used to kill her?"

"I had nothing to do with the *gadji*'s death!"

Andrei could see the lie written all over the older man. As a boy, he'd looked up to Milo, who'd seemed to be an honest and fair leader and a devoted father. He'd had such respect for Milo that he'd once told his mother that he wanted to be like him when he grew up.

He shuddered at the memory.

The last thing in the world he wanted was to be like the lying, quivering murderer before him.

Andrei continued to inch forward, while saying, "The murder weapon has been missing all these years. No wonder—you stashed it in the tree right where you killed Theresa Granville."

Milo appeared frantic when he said, "Andrei, you don't understand."

"What don't I understand, Milo? That you're capable of a crime of passion? Were you jealous of Carlo?" he asked, continuing to advance slowly, carefully. "Did you think you could have Theresa Granville for yourself?"

"No. It wasn't like that. I felt nothing for the *gadji* but—"

"Bastard!" Lizzie yelled, launching herself past Andrei and straight at Milo.

"Lizzie, no!"

Andrei tried to stop her. He was fast, but Milo was faster. Before Andrei's horrified eyes, the man yanked Lizzie against his body, levered an arm across her chest and held the knife blade to her throat.

"Stay back, Andrei, or I'll cut her. I swear I will!"

Andrei heard the words threatening the woman he loved, and through a haze of red, saw the knife at her throat.

Holding on tightly to his rage, he said, "You don't want to do this, Milo."

"I don't, Andrei, but you're forcing me to do it—you and your cousins and the *gadje* you've brought to our camp. All your poking and prodding has destroyed us. The carnival will never be the same!"

"The carnival isn't the same now, Milo. It hasn't been for ten years. It's tainted with the blood of Theresa Granville and now Valonia and God knows who else."

"Tony," Milo admitted, his eyes crazed. "He would have told...I couldn't let him...I can't let you...or her!"

The hand holding the knife was shaking with tension. As Andrei concentrated on the weapon, he sensed Milo's control slipping.

"Stop now!" Andrei told him. "Too many people know too much. You can't get away with this."

Milo licked his lips and shook his head. "I can," he said as if trying to convince himself. "I'll say it was Tony, that he's the murderer, that he was jealous of Carlo back then...and of you now. That he killed Valonia and put the letter in her hand. No one will be able to prove different. The alligators have got him by now." Milo adjusted the knife, tip to Lizzie's flesh, and Andrei felt his rage escalate as Milo said, "Like mother, like daughter."

"Nooooo!"

Andrei flung out his hand and the knife flew from Milo's with such force that it sunk hilt deep into the live oak and would take great strength to be pulled free.

Milo shoved Lizzie into him, and as Andrei caught her, she cried, "Don't let him get away!"

But the wily carnival owner had a head start, and Andrei knew that the man could quickly lose himself in the swamp. He wasn't about to let that happen. Concentrating on the limb of a cypress ahead on the path, Andrei brought it down right in front of Milo so that he got tangled in the branches. That stopped Milo long enough for Andrei to catch up to him. He tackled the man to the ground, where they rolled, one over the other.

The older man was amazingly strong and gave as good as he got. He traded punch for punch, though Andrei was so pumped he didn't feel the blows. Not until his back was turned to Milo and something came down on his head so hard he saw stars.

Dazed, he managed to stop himself from falling on his face.

Just enough time for Milo to get away.

ELIZABETH WAS at Andrei's side within seconds of his being hit with the very tree limb he'd brought down with is mind to stop the man. Milo had wielded the tree limb as if it weighed nothing, but she had a hard time moving it to free a stunned Andrei from the tangle of branches.

"Oh, Andrei, tell me you're all right," she begged as she gathered him in her arms. "Open your eyes and speak to me, please."

"Lizzie…" His lashes fluttered and lifted. "Milo?"

"He blindsided you and ran like the coward he is."

"We have to go after him."

He struggled against her, but she tried to keep him still, saying, "Not so fast. You're hurt. You might have a concussion."

But Andrei pushed himself up, anyway. "I can't let him get away." He shook his head as if to clear it, then winced.

Elizabeth winced, too. "Let the authorities see to him, Andrei," she pleaded.

But he wasn't listening to reason. "Which way? What if he hurts someone else before the authorities catch him?"

That decided it for her. Feeling sick inside, she pointed. "He went down that path."

"I can take it from here." Andrei was already moving off. "You go back, call Leon Thibault—"

"No! I'm not leaving you and don't bother arguing." She shadowed him. "Let's just keeping going before he disappears into the swamp."

"I'll find the bastard first."

They moved so swiftly Elizabeth was soon breathing hard. She didn't know how Andrei was doing it after being clocked with the tree limb. But he seemed steady enough. And as sure of himself as always. And determined.

Most of all determined.

He'd been like that as a teenager, she remembered, one of the reasons she'd been drawn to him. He'd known what he wanted and had set out to get it and the world be damned. One of the things he'd wanted had been her. Too bad he didn't still want her, she thought, remembering that he hadn't tried going further than kissing her.

Arriving at a landing, they stopped and looked out over the water. Elizabeth saw the silhouette of a small pirogue shooting up the bayou and of the man sitting in the shallow-hulled craft paddling furiously.

"Milo?" Elizabeth asked.

"That must be him." Andrei was on the move again. "We need to get out there before he disappears down one of the side channels."

"What? You mean swim out there?"

"I mean use one of those." He indicated two larger pirogues pulled up on the shore near the pier. He glanced back at her and said, "Don't worry, we're only going to borrow it." Then he slid it half into the water.

Elizabeth looked around, half-afraid that someone would see and accuse them of being thieves. Andrei jerked her into the flat-bottomed boat, which began to rock wildly as he pushed away from shore.

"Sit," he said as the pirogue swayed. "And stay still."

He climbed into the craft behind her, and a moment later they were off down the bayou, gliding deep into the swamp, cutting through the moonbeams that danced along the water, moving faster than she thought possible with only one person paddling.

Was Andrei doing it? she wondered.

Having seen the power of his mind for herself twice that night, she glanced back and checked his action with the double-bladed paddle. Fast, but not fast enough, she swore, to account for their speed.

For a while she thought they would catch up to Milo. The distance between the two boats dwindled by half. Then Milo turned down a channel so thick with cypress growth that their way grew jagged and filled with dark shadows.

"Can you see anything?" Andrei asked.

"A little. Up ahead I thought I saw movement to the right."

Where the channel split, Andrei followed the right branch. He relied on her for direction several times more, but eventually, the waterway narrowed and the growth multiplied until neither of them could see more than a yard or two beyond the prow. The slough was already drying up. Soon it would be overgrown, impossible to navigate until the winter's rain replenished it.

Andrei stopped paddling. His "We lost him" triggered Elizabeth's release valve.

Stress poured out of her in waves, until she could breathe normally again. She hadn't even realized how tight with dread she'd grown until this moment. Andrei might be the younger and stronger man, but Milo had years of illicit experience—dark paths he had followed to cover his crimes. He'd been desperate, ready to murder them both.

Carefully, Elizabeth turned around in the pirogue to face Andrei. Surprised when it didn't rock wildly, she realized the growth was so thick that it cradled them.

"Let the authorities pick him up, Andrei. Don't take any more chances, please. I don't want him to kill you."

Moonlight filtered through a break in the overgrowth and slashed across his features, which appeared puzzled to her.

"You sound as if you care what happens to me."

Elizabeth blinked and frowned at him. "Of course I care. I've always cared."

"Couldn't prove it by me," he said, sliding forward and nudging her so that she inched over, leaving him just enough room to squeeze in next to her. "One night you give the Gypsy boy a thrill ride. The next day he doesn't exist for you."

Thrill ride...

Yes, sharing the wonder of her own body for the first time had been more of a thrill than Elizabeth had expected. Remembering how she'd worried about her inexperience, she was thrilled to realize now that he'd found such pleasure in their union he still remembered it. But as for the rest...

"You didn't exist for me?" she said incredulously. "Is that what you thought?" Elizabeth closed her eyes. "Of course it was. How could you think otherwise?"

"Was it otherwise, Lizzie?" Andrei asked softly. He turned on his side and reclined next to her on the floor of the boat, trailed a finger up her arm until gooseflesh followed. "Tell me."

Her pulse was racing and her mouth went dry as she said, "My mother was murdered that same night, remember."

"I remember wanting to comfort you as soon as I heard. I came to see you, and you didn't want to be anywhere near me. So what was that?"

"Guilt. It was guilt, Andrei." Elizabeth turned and leaned on her elbow so that she could look at him directly when she explained, "I left my debutante ball and found you. If I hadn't, Mama might be alive today."

"Guilt. I sensed that," he admitted, "both then and now. I don't understand. Why? How does that follow?"

"She'd warned me about getting involved with you, told me nothing good could come of our seeing each other. Now I think she was really judging herself and thinking of her own decision to break it off with Carlo. At my ball, she and Daddy had a fight. It all started over his saying he would have to leave early, to drive to Baton Rouge where he had an early breakfast meeting. I didn't want to listen to any more but I caught the gist of the rest. Now I'm sure it was over Carlo, but at the time I didn't want to know. All I could think of was you, how you made me feel good about myself. How you made me smile, no matter what. I was upset and so I left in search of you. I'm sure Mama figured it out. No matter what had been going on between her and Carlo, I think on that particular night, Mama went to the carnival looking for me."

"All these years...you blamed yourself for her death?"

Elizabeth nodded. "I know differently now of course."

"Do you?"

He reached out to touch her face and she shivered. He'd always had this effect on her, ever since she could remember. Even when she'd fought him, she'd wanted him.

"I didn't mean to hurt you when I wouldn't see you," she whispered. "I loved you. But I loved Mama, too, and I was guilty and confused."

"You *loved* me?" He sounded disbelieving.

How could he have not known? she wondered.

"You were different from any other boy of my acquaintance," she told him. "You were...magical. Only I didn't know how magical until tonight, until you saved yourself on the Tilt-a-Whirl and then again with Milo. How?"

"Gypsy magic." He dipped his head and murmured in

her hair, "I don't know how. Some of us are born with gifts."

A concept that was difficult to accept, she thought, even as she echoed, "Gifts? Plural?"

His low laugh made the hair on her arms stand at attention. "Indeed."

"What, then?"

"Can't you guess?" he murmured, the timbre of his voice making her quake inside. "I know what women want. I can read you without even touching you, Lizzie, though touching you is better."

He gently swept the back of his fingers along the side of her face.

Elizabeth caught her breath, then let it out into a virtual explosion of air. "What *do* I want?"

"This." He trailed the fingers lower, down her neck. "And this." Then drew them forward along her collarbone and into the crevice between her breasts. "And this."

He kissed her long and deep, and when she thought she would gladly give up breathing if only he would keep kissing her forever, he stopped. A river of emotion shot through Elizabeth and she suddenly felt weepy.

"You're not going to cry, are you?" he asked, exactly as if he *could* read her emotions.

"No, of course not," she murmured, fighting the sting against the back of her eyelids.

"Then why are you suddenly filled with such strong feelings?"

"Daddy," she said, grabbing the first excuse she could find. "I was just thinking how relieved I am that he's not the one who killed Mama." Which of course was true.

"You had doubts?"

"Only ones created by other people. You. Miss Ina."

"I apologize for that."

"It isn't your fault."

"It is. I made you doubt your own father, partly because I couldn't see another motive...partly because I was still angry with you."

"Because I pulled away from you when you tried comforting me," she said, understanding now what she hadn't been able to understand then. "But that was ten years ago. And you never tried to see me again. You never came back."

"How can you be sure?"

"The following summer I waited and waited for the carnival to come. And when it did, I went looking for you only to be told that you wouldn't be back. That you were going to college and would become *gadje*, like your mother's people. I understand the school part, but it was summer. Why didn't you come back to the carnival for the summer?"

"Because of you," Andrei said. "I couldn't do it. I loved you, Lizzie, I'd loved you since you were a little girl. You were the reason I kept coming back. And then you were the reason I stayed away."

"And now? This time you didn't come back because of me."

He shook his head. "I came back despite you, because there were some things...personal problems...I had to work out. And, God help me, Lizzie, because I still love you."

He loved her still...Elizabeth frowned. "Why God help you?" Was he going to tell her he was committed to some other woman?

"Because there's nothing I can do about it," Andrei said, pulling away.

"I don't understand."

"More Gypsy magic. A curse, this," he said grimly "Valonia cursed the sons of those who put *her* only sor in prison. Wyatt Boudreaux, Garner Rousseau and me."

"What kind of curse?"

"The curse was different for each of us. *Justice is blind. Love is death. The law is impotent.*"

A shiver ran up Elizabeth's spine. "Wyatt lost his sight on the job, but now he has it back, right? I don't really know much about Garner."

"For years, anyone he cared about died."

"But doesn't he love your cousin Sabina? She's all right, isn't she?"

Andrei nodded. "Though it was a close call. She almost died healing Garner."

"But both men have worked through their curses. What about you? How did Valonia curse you?"

Andrei didn't say anything. A taut connection wired between them, and suddenly Elizabeth understood.

"Oh," she whispered.

"So you see why my loving you does neither of us any good," he said bitterly.

"It does *me* good, Andrei. It does my heart good. As for the rest…I don't care about some damn Gypsy curse!" Those tears were welling up in her eyes again, but this time she didn't care. She reached out and touched him, running her fingertips along the beard stubble covering his cheek and jaw. "I've been so lonely for you all these years, Andrei. I've been unhappy deep down in the darkest reaches of my soul, but all that's changed in the last few days. With you, I feel alive again. Please don't deny me—I'll take whatever you have to give."

He caught her wrist and burned a kiss into it until Elizabeth felt faint. When he released it, she slid her hand behind his head and hooked him by the neck so that when she rolled back, he rolled with her.

"Lizzie…"

"No protests. Kiss me, Andrei. Kiss me like you love me."

HE REALLY DID LOVE Lizzie, Andrei decided, impassioned by the thought, now more than ever. He tried to tell her so in a kiss that seared his soul.

Her generosity—telling him she wanted whatever he had to give—touched him deeply.

Even as he kissed her, as his body responded—just as it always did, only to disappoint him at the crucial moment—Andrei knew he was being selfish. He couldn't give Lizzie what she needed…and he couldn't stop himself from trying. But he wouldn't let her go unsatisfied, and he would have the memory to last him a lifetime. It would have to, for no matter her protests, he couldn't allow her to share his curse. In his heart he knew that while he would always love her, the fair thing for him to do was let her go.

He touched her breasts through the dress and felt her nipples spring forth to kiss his palms. He groaned into her mouth and explored lower, past her belly and her thighs, scooping up the material of her skirt and finding her flesh.

Lizzie moaned and spread her thighs and Andrei's erection grew.

He wanted her more than anything he'd ever wanted in his life. Dipping a finger beneath her panties, he found her wet and ready for him. Hand trembling, he tugged them down below her hips. She helped him slide the panties down her legs and kick them aside. Then her hands found him. Her touch through the denim was exquisite, and he held his breath as she unzipped the jeans and slid her hands inside.

"Lizzie," he breathed, heartsick at knowing that any second now, his erection would fade as it had so many times before he'd given up trying. "Stop."

Tugging at his waistband and pulling it down over his hips, she didn't seem to be listening. Andrei closed his eyes and prepared himself for the moment when he would disappoint her. He would make it up to her, though, he vowed, even as he felt light kisses across his stomach. He groaned and arched and suddenly he was surrounded by a wet, warm mouth.

"Lizzie…"

Her mouth worked magic. He grew harder, tauter, closer to release than he'd been in years.

He couldn't help but take what pleasure he could. His fingers tangled in her hair and he moved against her. She had a clever mouth that kept him hard and aching for her. But he wanted other things, too. Closeness. Warmth. For, in reality, he'd missed that more than anything.

Groaning, he pulled Lizzie up so that he could kiss that clever mouth of hers. While he was doing so, she straddled him and shifted so that he felt her wet entrance against his tip. Unable to help himself, he pushed and the tip parted her silky lips.

Rather than failing as he'd done in the past, he slid right into Lizzie as if he belonged there.

"What have you done to me?" he murmured in her hair.

"*Gadji* magic," she whispered, levering her hands against his chest and rocking over him.

Andrei slid a hand between them. He paid homage to her breasts, released them from the dress and bra so that he could kiss them and suckle them. Dipping a hand lower, he explored beneath her skirts until he found her center. She made a low noise deep in the back of her throat and arched. An increase in pressure, and she began to move faster and harder. He followed the beat with his fingers until she began to shudder.

"Now, Lizzie," he urged, watching her face in the moonlight. "Come for me now!"

She cried out and went still, and his erection began to pulse—the beginning of the little death he hadn't been able to capture for years. No orgasm had ever been longer in coming, he vowed, or as sweet.

When he pulled her back to him, Lizzie was still shuddering. Andrei wrapped his arms around the woman he loved and held her against his heart.

Somehow the curse had been broken.

Chapter Seven

Heat woke Elizabeth. Not the heat of the morning, because it was still too early. Andrei's heat. His body was spooned around hers and he'd thrown an arm around her waist.

She slipped out from under the constriction and scooted away the few inches available to her. The boat was cramped, but she hadn't minded. They hadn't needed much room to make love in the dark of night.

But it was daylight, or would be soon.

Morning crept over the horizon like a forbidden lover. Elizabeth would have liked to creep away with it. Uncertainty filled her, and a glance at Andrei made her stomach knot. A miracle had happened between them—his curse had been broken. She remembered every word spoken in passion. She remembered every touch.

But she also remembered that night ten years before.

What if the morning brought her the same results, if in a different manner? She knew the carnival would be packed up today and gone tomorrow.

The last time, she had been the one to turn Andrei away. But no matter what he'd said about loving her, he hadn't fought for her, hadn't tried to chase away her doubts. After learning about her mother's death, she'd been in shock. And, in her mind, she could only believe that he'd been glad for the excuse to go.

What if she'd been right?

And so, as if it was her very last chance, she drank in the sight of the man she loved. A sight that might have to last her a lifetime.

The lashes brushing his cheeks fluttered open and his dark gaze found hers. His lips curled into a smile.

"Morning," he murmured.

"Morning," she returned, her smile feeling brittle. He reached for her, but she backed off, saying, "We should get on our way and make that call to Leon Thibault."

Andrei's smile faded, but he didn't argue, simply sat up and slid back to where he'd set the paddle. Elizabeth was both relieved and disappointed. She could have used some reassurances, rather than renewed strain between them.

Andrei used the paddle like a pole and shoved them back from the growth in which the pirogue had become tangled. She reached over and pushed against a cypress knee, then whipped her hand away when something slithered into the swamp nearby. A fat brown cottonmouth.

The journey back seemed fraught with danger. What looked to be logs in the dark became, in the morning light, sluggish alligators that opened their mouths and gulped air as they passed. At the shoreline, No Tresspassing! signs warned intruders to stay in their boats.

She kept her attention on the swamp so she wouldn't have to think too deeply about what came next with Andrei. They churned through floating hyacinths, with mullet and shad leaping before the boat. And a festive line of red ribbons trailed into the bush, a track for inexperienced bullfrog hunters to follow.

When they arrived back at the dock, the other large

pirogue was gone—fishermen started work early—and she wondered if an alert had already gone up about this one being stolen.

Andrei got out first and tied up the boat, then held out his hand to her.

Gazing up at his face, she couldn't read him. Still, she took his hand and let him help her onto the dock. They stood there a moment, a breath apart—she with her eyes averted, waiting for him to say something that would dispel the chill that had more to do with her own uncertainty than the weather.

"Let's stay together," he said. "I don't want anything happening to you."

Not exactly romantic, but reassuring nevertheless.

Elizabeth figured they were halfway back to the live oak before she asked, "Do you think they'll have trouble finding Milo? He could be far from here by now."

"He would never leave Florica on her own," Andrei said. "He would come back for her, may have already. And the carnival is his. Who knows what he might be planning?" he mused. "Don't let down your guard."

Elizabeth took the warning seriously, but nothing untoward happened. As they approached the grounds, however, mechanical noises got her attention.

"What is that?"

"The men are breaking down the rides. We were to be on the move tomorrow at daylight."

Elizabeth swallowed hard. Andrei would be on the move, too. Then what? He still didn't offer any reassurances.

As they cut across the carnival grounds, the noise suddenly stopped, only to be replaced by a cacophony of voices. And in the distance, a crowd gathered.

"Something is going on," Andrei murmured, hurrying off.

Elizabeth kept up, and in a moment they were at the edge of a crowd gathered around the Tilt-a-Whirl. It wasn't until they broke through the crush of bodies that Elizabeth recognized the two detectives. One was bending over something. Someone. A body. She pushed in closer and saw Milo Vasilli lying sprawled across the floor of the Tilt-a-Whirl, his eyes staring, his mouth open as if in a scream.

And protruding from his chest...the knife that had killed her mother.

"I DON'T BELIEVE Milo committed suicide," Andrei said in protest to Leon Thibault's explanation. "Too damn tidy!"

And he was certain that the knife that killed the carnival owner was the one from the live oak—he recognized the handle. Even as strong as Milo had been, it would have been some feat for him to have freed the damn thing.

"Be careful with that," Andrei cautioned the examiner who'd pulled the knife from the body and was dropping it into a bag. Old, long-dried blood that he hadn't noticed before spattered the handle. "It's evidence—"

Thibault stepped in. "Don't stick your nose where it don't belong, Sobatka. Of course it's evidence—"

"—in Theresa Granville's murder," Andrei finished.

"What?"

"We saw Milo pull that knife from a hollow in the live oak where Theresa Granville's body was found. Take a good look at that handle. Dried blood."

"That doesn't mean anything."

The D.A. appeared disbelieving until Andrei explained what had happened the night before.

Thibault looked from him to Lizzie. "That your story, too?" he asked her.

"Yes. He all but admitted to murdering Mama. I'm afraid you're going to have to stop a certain execution," she said.

"I see." But he didn't sound convinced. "We'll have to go over the story again, get all the details in writing."

"Of course," Andrei said, wondering what Lizzie was thinking.

The carnies were disbursing, keeping busy, going back to dismantling rides and tents, their mood dark, their future uncertain. Her gaze darted around as if she was afraid to look at anything or anyone too long. Especially him.

Was she already regretting sleeping with him? It seemed so.

Or maybe she was just freaked out by this latest development. Milo dead. Murdered. By whom?

"I'll have one of the men bring you back to my office in Les Baux," Thibault was saying.

"I would like to go home and get cleaned up first." Lizzie was fidgeting, as though she couldn't wait to leave. "I can get myself there."

Because of Milo? Andrei wondered. Or because she wanted to get away from him. "Give me a minute and I'll take you."

But she was already backing off. "That won't be necessary."

Andrei pressed his lips together lest he argue the point. She was safe from Milo. She wanted to put some distance between them, that was obvious.

And before he could convince her to wait, Thibault mused, "What would make someone kill Milo Vasilli?"

Distracted long enough for Lizzie to turn and flee before he could speak, Andrei tried not to take it personally.

This was a difficult time for her, he told himself. He would give her some space, but he wouldn't disappear, not until he was certain that was what she wanted.

The D.A. went on, his sharp gaze going from carny to carny. "Which of these seemingly grief-stricken people is, in fact, a murderer?"

Andrei snapped back to him for a moment. "Maybe you ought to be looking at who *isn't* here."

CAUGHT UP in an emotional whirlwind, Elizabeth averted her gaze from the signs of the carnival leaving. She didn't need to see the rides being dismantled or the tents being taken down to know that it was over.

Not just the carnival, but her and Andrei.

She crossed the grounds as quickly as she could, and it was only when she came to the path—a shortcut home—that she slowed and mentally began to process Milo's death. Most significant—at least she thought so— was the murder weapon. Whoever had removed it from the trunk had been really strong. Milo himself? She supposed a crazed person might have more adrenaline and therefore more strength than normal, and Milo certainly had been crazed the night before.

But for all these years, Milo had left the murder weapon hidden. What in the world would make him bring it back to the carnival? And why would someone else use it to kill him, unless…

Unless the same person who killed Milo was involved in the attempts on the lives of Andrei's cousins and their lovers. Why? Because that someone must have been involved in her mother's murder, Elizabeth concluded.

Thinking she ought to go back and offer that theory to Leon Thibault, she hesitated. She would have to face Andrei, as well, and she wasn't sure she was ready for that.

And then she heard a noise behind her that raised the hairs on the back of her neck.

Someone was following her!

Her pulse rushed and so did she, straight for home.

But suddenly other sounds, these somewhere ahead, made her falter. Heart pounding into her throat—what if the murderer were after *her* now?—she looked around wildly and left the path, cutting off into the brush.

The scrunch of footfalls seemed to surround her.

Frightened and confused, Elizabeth realized she'd turned herself around and didn't know in what direction to go. Where the hell was she?

Suddenly someone stepped into her path and she nearly jumped out of her skin. And then she saw who it was.

"Florica." Tension whooshed right out of her. "Lord, you startled me."

The child-woman giggled softly, and as if playing a game, she said, "You're it!" Then just as quickly, Florica's good humor disappeared. Her smile faded, leaving an angry visage and cold eyes staring at Elizabeth.

And why not? Florica had just lost a parent to violence.

"I know how you must be feeling," Elizabeth said reassuringly. "I lost my mother the way you just lost your father. I'm so sorry about everything, Florica."

"You're sorry?" She seemed puzzled. "Truly?"

"That your father was murdered so horribly? Of course."

Florica's confused expression only lasted a moment. Then she shook her head and said, "Papa had to die. He tried to hurt Andrei. I saw him. I saw you, too, touching Andrei and kissing him. You shouldn't have done that."

Elizabeth's spine crawled. "I shouldn't have?" she echoed as she tried to think. Slowly, she backed away.

A solemn Florica shook her head. "Andrei was mine. Just like Carlo."

"C-Carlo?"

"He was going to take me to the movies. But then he didn't come and I saw him with the *gadji*." Florica focused on Elizabeth. "She looked like you."

"Mama? What do you know about her? What did you have to do with her? Theresa Granville—that is who you mean, isn't it?"

"Theresa Granville," Florica echoed, nodding. "She gave me a letter for Carlo, but I read it and then I knew that Carlo had betrayed me with her. She was bad, a *gadji* harlot, Papa called her. I knew what I had to do then."

Elizabeth blinked and tried to take this in. Florica was more a child than a woman mentally, but she undoubtedly had a woman's needs. She'd thought Carlo had cared for her and then had cheated on her...and she'd what?

"Did you tell Milo—your papa—about Carlo?"

"After. He kept me safe."

The truth couldn't be clearer. "Then Milo didn't do it," Elizabeth murmured, more for her own satisfaction than Florica's. "He wasn't the murderer, after all."

"Papa took care of me. But he's gone now. What will I do?" Florica asked in her little-girl voice. She frowned and struggled with her skirts. "I'll think about it when the carnival is on the road again."

The Gypsy freed her hand from the garment, and in it, she held a knife that looked every bit as deadly as the one that had killed Mama and Milo. Sweat beaded Elizabeth's brow as she realized she was facing not only a murderer, but one who'd been crazed enough to have the strength to pull free a knife that had been hilt-deep in a tree.

Chapter Eight

Watching and listening as the scenario unfolded, Andrei reacted the moment he saw the knife. Florica grabbed Lizzie's wrist with her free hand, and though Lizzie struggled, she couldn't break the hold. And no matter how hard Andrei concentrated, he couldn't repeat his performance with Milo.

The telekinesis wouldn't work on Florica.

Something about the way her out-of-sync brain worked made her and the things around her resistant to any kind of Gypsy magic.

When he cut through the growth to get to them, Florica's eyes widened. "Andrei!"

Not wanting her to panic the way Milo had, he calmly said, "Florica, did you forget you were supposed to meet me?"

"What?"

Lizzie looked around, wide-eyed. He sensed her terror, but for the moment, he had to ignore it and concentrate on Florica.

"The movie, remember?" He could only hope her mind skittered through time and fooled her. "I was going to take you to see a movie. You changed your hair for me."

Confusion crossed her features for a moment, then she muttered, "Carlo, not you."

But a moment was all he'd needed to close the gap, saying, "Put down the knife!"

"Not until its work is done," Florica said, raising it.

Lizzie struggled to free herself. "Andrei, don't!"

But Andrei stepped in front of the woman he loved, shielding her from the instrument of death. As the knife sliced into him, hot pain seared his left shoulder.

"Andrei!" both women screamed at once.

Heedless of the blood gushing from his shoulder, he grabbed for Florica's knife-hand, but she was too quick for him. She let go of Lizzie and backed off, while wildly waving the knife.

"Stay away from her," Lizzie whispered. "She killed her own father."

"I got that." To the child-woman who was staring at his bleeding shoulder and sobbing, he said, "Put down the knife, Florica. I know you didn't mean to hurt me."

"I *didn't* mean to hurt you. I love you. I loved Carlo. I loved Papa, too." She shook her head. "Now I have no one. Papa can't protect me anymore and I have no one left to love."

Even without use of his gift, Andrei sensed what her terror would force her to do. He lunged to stop her, but again Florica was faster, plunging the blade into her own chest.

"My God!" Lizzie cried, as brilliant red bloomed across Florica's white cotton blouse.

Too late. Andrei shook his head as the young woman he'd befriended crumpled to the ground. Just then, Leon Thibault burst into the clearing with two uniformed policemen at his side.

Andrei stooped down as Florica whispered, "Papa, I'm coming," and her life's blood pumped out of her chest.

"So, you were right, Sobatka," Thibault said, signaling the uniforms to take over.

"Unfortunately," Andrei agreed, rising.

The policemen bent over Florica, but she'd already gone still, her eyes open and staring.

Andrei turned and shielded Lizzie from the sight.

She gasped. "Your shoulder!" She immediately began ripping her skirt. "You need a doctor..."

"I'll be fine."

Bunching the cloth, she pressed it to his wound, and from her drawn, pale face and her frightened-for-him expression—not to mention the fact that he eavesdropped on her emotions—Andrei knew exactly how Miss Elizabeth Granville felt about her Gypsy lover.

"I COULDN'T HAVE endured losing you, too," Elizabeth admitted later, after a trip to the emergency room.

Andrei would be fine—his had been little more than a flesh wound, more blood than lasting damage, thank God. As soon as his wound had been cleaned and bandaged, he'd insisted on leaving the hospital. He'd even insisted on seeing her to her front door.

Now he moved forward, pinning her against a porch pillar.

"Your shoulder," she cautioned.

"It hurts horribly," he said, his tone sexy.

"And there's only one thing I can think of to make it feel better."

Then Andrei kissed her, one of those slow, deep kisses that made her knees weak. Elizabeth clung to him, careful of his shoulder.

When he drew back, he murmured, "You're never going to lose me. Not if I have anything to say about it."

Her heart skipped a couple of beats. "You mean you'll return to Les Baux with the carnival every year?" Assuming the carnival didn't fall into ruins now that its fate was undecided.

He stroked her cheek with the back of his hand. "I love you, Lizzie, and I never want to live without you again. I was hoping for a more permanent relationship."

Dizzy with relief, she quickly said, "I love you, too, Andrei. And if you want me to work the midway with you, I will! I could sell tickets or—"

"Shh." He put a finger to her lips. "I didn't mean that."

"Oh."

"What I'm trying to say…is that won't be necessary. My engineering background can be put to better use in a new job. I rejoined the carnival this summer to hide from my curse, but I no longer have a reason to hide—thanks to you."

"If you want my opinion, you have yourself to thank," Lizzie said. "There had to be more to its end than my loving you. I've loved you all along."

"Then what?"

"You saved Carlo. You put yourself in danger to do that…and to protect me." She looked skyward. "I think Valonia knows what you and Wyatt and Garner all did to free her son, and she freed you in return." Her heart was so full that she could hardly believe it. "So, you want to get *gadje* work again. In Les Baux?"

He laughed. "I was thinking of going back to New Orleans…unless there's something keeping you here."

"Only Daddy." Lest he mistake her meaning, she

quickly added, "But I'm sure he'll look forward to our visits."

"We can have any life we decide on. Together."

Together.

The word thrilled her as did Andrei when he picked her up despite her protests and carried her inside, all the while whispering how she would now get a real taste of his Gypsy magic.

Epilogue

Breathing in his unexpected freedom, Carlo Mustov was grateful to be part of the day's proceedings, pleased to honor those who had risked their lives to prove him innocent. To free him.

The transition from prison to normal life after so many years hadn't been easy, but he was back where he belonged. A member of his clan. Part of the carnival in which they all now had an interest. All familiar and beloved. The outside world could wait until he was ready for it.

For now, he wanted to concentrate on happy things. On happy people. His looking from one expectant couple to the second to the third, drove away uncertainty, at least for the moment.

They had all married in *gadje* ceremonies over the past several months—Alessandra King and Wyatt Boudreaux, Sabina King and Garner Rousseau, Andrei Sobatka and Elizabeth Granville. And now that the carnival had shut down for the winter, the clan had returned to Les Baux for the *abiav,* the simple ceremony that would join each of the couples' lives in Romany tradition.

Some of the townspeople had joined them, as well. Not Richard Granville of course. For that, Carlo Mustov was glad. He didn't want to see his old rival and was certain Elizabeth's father felt the same way.

But he hadn't killed Theresa, and now everyone knew that.

He couldn't believe that Florica had murdered the woman he'd loved, and in a way, he blamed himself. He'd cared for Florica as he might a little sister. That she'd read more into his affection for her had never occurred to him. Had he been more astute, he might have prevented the tragedy that had affected all their lives.

But not all bad had come from it, he thought, as he approached the couples. The men were beaming, the women radiant. All wore the colorful dress of the Romany. No pale wedding garments here, he thought, but colors as strong and as bright as the young women themselves.

"You make me so proud," Carlo told his cousins.

He kissed Alessandra's cheek, then Sabina's. He stopped before Elizabeth Granville, who reminded him so much of her late mother. When he started to turn away, she put a hand on his arm and looked at him expectantly. He kissed her cheek, too, and when she smiled at him, unshed tears burned his eyes.

Carlo then picked up a basket of bread, and each bride and each groom took a piece. Next, he handed Andrei a ceremonial dagger, which was passed from one to the other, each person using the sharp point to prick a finger and let a drop of blood stain the bread. When all six had finished, the brides and grooms exchanged bread with their partners and ate.

A cheer from the clan went up, and Carlos said, "You are now joined together forever. Feast!"

A whole pig and several fowl had been roasting over an open fire. Along with the meat, huge platters of fried potatoes and boiled cabbage stuffed with rice and herbs and garlic were passed around the tables.

But Carlo's favorite part was afterward, when the appetite for food was sated and that for romance began. Musicians played traditional rhythmic tunes, and the couples wrapped their arms around each other as if they would never let go, and they danced.

Carlo watched contentedly, then dreamed a little, imagining the woman he'd loved was in his arms once more. After all these years, after all the horror of her death and his own imprisonment, he still thought of her often, and now that he'd seen her letter to him at last, her words would be burned into his memory forever.

No matter what happens, I will always love you…

No Gypsy magic would bring Theresa Granville back, but she was avenged at last, and she would live on his heart.

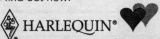

$ **Saving Money Has Never Been This Easy!** $

Just fill out and send in this form from any October, November and December 2002 books and we will send you a coupon booklet worth a total savings of $20.00 off future purchases of Harlequin and Silhouette books in 2003.

Yes! It's that easy!

I accept your incredible offer!
Please send me a coupon booklet:

Name (PLEASE PRINT)

Address   Apt. #

City   State/Prov.   Zip/Postal Code

**In a typical month, how many
Harlequin and Silhouette novels do you read?**

❑ **0-2**   ❑ **3+**

097KJKDNC7   097KJKDNDP

Please send this form to:
In the U.S.: Harlequin Books, P.O. Box 9071, Buffalo, NY 14269-9071
In Canada: Harlequin Books, P.O. Box 609, Fort Erie, Ontario L2A 5X3

Allow 4-6 weeks for delivery. Limit one coupon booklet per household. Must be postmarked no later than January 15, 2003.

HARLEQUIN®
Makes any time special®

Silhouette®
Where love comes alive™

© 2002 Harlequin Enterprises Limited   PHQ402

HARLEQUIN®
INTRIGUE®

A royal family in peril...
A kingdom in jeopardy...
And only love can save them!

THE CROWN
AFFAIR

Continues in November 2002 with

ROYAL RANSOM
BY SUSAN KEARNEY

In the second exciting installment in
THE CROWN AFFAIR trilogy, Princess Tashya's baby
brothers have been kidnapped. With no time to lose,
Her Royal Highness sets out to save the young princes,
whether her family—or the dangerously seductive
CIA agent hired to protect her—liked it or not!

Coming in December 2002:
ROYAL PURSUIT

Look for these exciting new stories
wherever Harlequin books are sold!

HARLEQUIN®
Makes any time special ®